The Secret Of The Stars

Written By

Gitz Crazyboy

Cover Illustrated by

Alyssa M. General

ISBN: 1543195075
ISBN-13: 978-1543195071

FOR KEELAN

CONTENTS

ACKNOWLEDGMENTS

To all those that I have loved and lost and those that are still kicking around. To my mother who read me to sleep almost every night as a child, planting seeds of adventures that took root in my dreams. My Beautiful Indigenous culture to which I am truly nothing without.

PROLOGUE

Do you remember the first place you called home? You've got to think hard and remember way back, even before you could walk or talk or breathe. I know it's difficult but you have to try. Do you remember the home you lived in before you were even born? No. Well I don't expect you to; seldom does anyone ever remember that beautiful magical place.

The first home you had before you were born was within the womb of your mother. Try not to forget it.

Do you remember that sacred place you came from before you were here and took home within the womb of your mother? No? Well I don't blame you for that either, even less of us can remember that divine place, it's called the Sky World. It exists and it's as real as the voice you hear that is talking to you right now.

Word for word you will forget this story and over time when you look back you'll only remember fragments. Just as you live your life day by day you will forget the Sky World. What it looks like, how it smells and most importantly what it feels like.

In the beginning your soul waits at the edge of the Sky World.

What is the Sky World you ask? It is a sunless moonless lands that stretches out beyond the heavens above. It's the pathway

1

where stars both begin and end. There your spirit looks down at the wonder of this planet, marvelling in the splendour that is all life. Your spirit sits at the edge of darkness waiting for a bridge that will connect it to our world here. But even when a bridge is present it still waits just a little bit longer, spirits need a vessel to travel while it explores life, it needs a body.

The sky world is where you come from and when you pass on it is where you will return.

The bridge from the Sky World is formed from something incredible. Your Mother and Father thought and more importantly dreamed about the miracle of having a baby. You were first conceived in the part of the brain that creates thoughts and dreams. Before you came into this world, you were nothing more than a beautiful wish. It was that wish that crafted and shaped the bridge between our worlds.

Traveling from the sky world to this world is a gift. But I am getting a bit ahead of myself here, so let me begin again.

THE FOUR

In my earliest memories, I'm looking at my hands and they were tiny. I remember struggling to pick up these wooden blocks. I remember reaching out and stretching and focusing just to grab a toy train. I can faintly recall how I perceived the world but what I remember is that everything had a novelty because everything felt new and everything was innocent. Looking at the world through a child's eyes all things are amazing because all things are beautiful. I used to give everything a personality back then from toys to doors. Some of my toys were good toys and some of the most random things around the house were bad things, like a tea cup that had a chip in it.

I remember back when I wasn't very much older than you. I lived and grew up on a tiny little Blackfoot reservation. It was constantly windy regardless of what season it was, winter, summer, spring or fall. It was so bad that birds couldn't ever fly against the wind no matter how hard they beat their wings they just stayed in one place. And when they gave up flapping the wind just took them away, I'd wager it must have blown them clear out of the province.

My rez was far away from the cities, the towns and even the forests; it was away from almost all civilization. It was a place out in the prairies and the foothills and just a few miles from the Rocky Mountains. I had a cousin who said he once won a rock throwing contest the reservation held cause he threw one that sailed all the way to and across the mountains. He later admitted to fooling the people on our rez saying it was just a really small bird that looked like a rock that he threw and said the wind carried it.

The only real thing connecting us to the rest of the world was a highway and train tracks that were always frequented with busy travelers. People were always going here to there and seldom stopping to visit or explore our little reservation. Some people on my rez seemed to live and die there doing the same nothings day, after day, after day. Some people believed they would never leave the rez. They believed that they were stuck to it and bound to it and over the course of their lives they would prove this belief true.

But I got to tell you my rez has the most beautiful scenery; the mountains were always in the horizon to the west and during the summer seasons all you could see for miles around were rolling hills with tall flowing blades of golden grass.

However, this story doesn't begin during the summer, no this was during a bitterly cold winter. And, I was home carefully tucked away from the harsh winds that come with the season. When I begin to think back, I mean really think hard, this tale begins at one of my earliest memories. With me watching the Television...

While my mother (your Grandmother) would be doing housework and chores throughout the week, she would often sit me down to watch 'Educational Programming'. Usually 'Educational Programming' had puppets that talked to you of the environment and the world around. On that particular day I was learning about the words starting with the letter "C" from a yellow monster with purple horns. The monster, although he didn't sound like a monster because most monsters sound scary due to an incredible buildup of phlegm in their mouth and throat. This monster didn't snarl or growl or howl, he sounded more like a high-pitched harmless goat.

"C" he said "Stands for Change".

Out of nowhere a gang of monkeys took over the screen and started to fight while jumping around and throwing bananas at each other. God I love monkeys they look like little mischievous hairy people with tails! These particular ones were dressed like pirates. One of the monkeys looked at the monster and said.

"Does Banana start with C?"

And the monster replied.

"No. Banana starts with the letter B."

"Well you know what starts with the letter C?"

"What?"

"Catch!"

And then he threw a banana at the monsters face. I've always wanted to catch a monkey and make him my best friend. Everybody has a dog or a cat, I wanted my animal to be a monkey. Then the monkeys on the screen went from throwing bananas to throwing pies and soon after were throwing water balloons.

But right in the middle of all this a blue puppet dressed in an expensive brown suit with a brown moustache with almost no hair on his balding brown head popped up on the screen and said to me.

"Sonny boy, come close to the T.V.!"

"My names not Sonny."

"My apologizes young sir. Come here!"

I was stunned the television was talking to me. In utter disbelief I took one baby step towards the screen.

"No silly, come closer than that"

I stopped, frozen in shock – he could really see me.

"I promise I won't bite. Look I got no teeth." He said as he opened his mouth revealing nothing but gums. He even put his hand into his mouth and bit down as hard as he could.

"See! No teeth marks." As he proudly showed me his hand without the faintest hint of indents.

I was looking at him in disbelief still not moving.

"I'm not supposed to be doing this because you never

know whose listening but I swear on the blood of the moon I won't hurt ya!" He promised.

"Moons can bleed?" I asked

"Anything can bleed." He responded

I walked towards the screen.

"Now listen closely, I've got a major important tip top secret that I want to share with you. But I absolutely positively need to know that you can keep a secret?"

As I moved my head closer to the television I nodded yes.

"I mean it's really a big thing, I don't know if I should even tell you such a crazy spectacular amazing thing. So, I have to ask you again, can I trust that you'll keep it?"

I nodded my head harder and faster I really wanted to know I hated not knowing secrets or being left out of the loop.

"Are you a 100 percent sure?"

My eyes widened as I shook my head even faster, it was no longer a want. It was a need, the same kind of need you have when you really have to go to the bathroom to pee.

"Oooook, I'll only tell you because I like ya kid. Look, tonight there's going to be a colossal meteor shower. This hasn't happened for very, very long time. Do you know what colossal means?"

I shook my head no. I had no idea what it meant but colossal sounded like a fancy word.

"Colossal means extremely large and that means there's going to be <u>Hundreds</u> and <u>Thousands</u> of shooting stars and they will be running and dancing across the night sky. This won't happen again for a very, very long time…well, maybe when you're a grumpy old man with white hair and no teeth, maybe then you'll get lucky enough to see it. But then again, what if you never get the chance to see it? Why this could be your one and only chance! Do you want to see it? Cause you know if you don't. I could always just tell someone else who would probably love to watch it instead."

I was totally sold on this colossal meteor shower thing and smiling as I said "Yes!" I loved knowing a good secret and I loved being in the loop.

"Ok, but you've got to stay up late."

The blue, balding puppet man leaned close to the television screen raised his hand to cover part of his mouth looking around as he whispered to me.

"...You're going to have to stay up late; way past your bed time. Just know that sometimes magic can happen on nights like these."

That night, I had to pretend to fall asleep as my mother put me to bed. I shut my eyes and got all curled up. She gave me a kiss like she always did and left the room. As she left I opened my eyes and waited to hear her walk to her room down the hall and close the door. When I heard it shut I jumped up as quietly as I could I silently walked over and began looking out my window. I sat and waited, And Waited, AND WAITED. I was shaking my head to stay awake, slapping myself and splashing cold water into my face. Time began to drag as I looked at my wall clock. The second hand was moving slower and slower and then it completely froze. I didn't know about the unnatural effects that magic has on our world and on us. You never really know the magic has got you, until it has you in its grasp. Unbeknownst to me or anyone else before they hear it but there's an enchanting world just out there on the edge of the horizon. Some place between, imagination, dreams and life.

I was waiting for what seemed to be ages for those hundreds and thousands of shooting stars just like the puppet man on the television said. Instead those stars were just sitting motionless out in the night's sky not even bothering to moving an inch. I remember my mother, telling me "Sometimes people lie or fib to make things better than they seem."

Disappointment steadily grew inside it was that same feeling you get when unwrapping a Christmas present that you know in your heart of what it has to be. You write to Santa, tell the big guy what you want and do your best to behave. Then as the last shred of paper is pulled on the present you've been asking for all year and as the box is being opened something completely different is inside and sadly it's an unwanted thing. That's the kind of disappointment that kills hope and I could feel that disappointment growing inside. Maybe the puppet did in fact lie to me.

So, I gave up hope on the stars and I was about to give in to sleep. I walked away from the window and jumped into bed. But, just as I was laying to rest with my head about to touch my pillow and just before my eyelids closed. I saw through the window, four stars in the shape of a diamond brighten up vividly side by side. Those four stars that were floating and shinning began to vibrate, moments before it seemed like they were nothing out of the ordinary. One true fact they don't teach you in schools is that stars aren't just stars they are all 'extraordinary'. They're just hiding out there in the universe until the right kind of night with the right kind of magic arrives just so they can uncloak their secret. They waited on that night for no other wandering eyes to be gazing up at the heavens, because on that night they were waiting for me. Each of the four were getting ready to run and dance and play crossing the night's sky. I was unaware as I sat there looking up at them that my whole life they were always looking down and watching over me. Then one by one they fell to the earth.

One fell to the North.

One fell to the East.

One fell to the South.

And the Last One fell to the West.

Each fell past the horizon further than I could see and as they hit the earth they lit up the sky. Suddenly and abruptly my eyes became heavy so heavy that I couldn't keep them open anymore. I yawned long and loudly and became very eager to enter the world of nocturnes. I had been hit by a sleeping spell. Even if I wanted to fight the sleep I couldn't. I closed my eyes my head hit the pillow and this was my dream...

DREAMS AND STORIES

I remember being outside of my house in the cold of winter. In front of me was a single red willow bush and on that willow bush was a giant blue and black cocoon. As I walked towards it, the cocoon began to pulsate in and out like it was breathing. Then a slit ripped open and continued down on one side and from it a beautiful red and black and white wing emerged. A giant butterfly the size of my head crawled out. It beat its wings and each time it did my eyes began to shut from the wind.

When I opened them, I was sitting down outside of a single red 2 storey house with a nice white picket fence which rested on top of a hill. It wasn't winter nor was it cold. Through one of the windows of the house I could see a variety of paints and colours, but they were splashed everywhere, on the floors, the walls even the roof, it looked like such a big mess. My arms were tied to my body, I hated being tied up it always got me restless. In some of my scarier dreams, I am tied up in a room that is on fire and I need to get untied to get out. But this wasn't a scary dream. I was restless and what made me more restless was seeing my toy trains lying down in front of me. It took some scrambling, but I finally freed myself. I grabbed my toy trains and began crashing them into each other over and over again. I heard a commotion as I looked up and seen two giant black birds one was a Raven and the smaller one was a Crow. I could feel that the smaller one was nice and funny and the other one I think was his brother. He was bigger and his feathers were ruffled and had a tinge of red within them and he also just looked mean.

"Caw, Caw, Caw" cawed the Crow bobbing his head up and down looking up at the Raven and then looking at me. "Hmmm, Nosey kid." The Raven spoke English that was clear as day. "Let's send him back and on his way." Snapped the Mean Raven.

"CAWCAWCAWCAWCAW." The crow said jumping up and down

"Oh shut up and mind your own business... You'll end up blabbing about everything, you're always telling everyone about the truth behind the enigma's we present. And you know what that means?" Asked the Mean Raven

"CAW?" Stammered the Crow

"They stop thinking for themselves and you kill the medicine! People need those mysteries because they need to search and find meaning." Snarled the Raven
This dream world I was in, existed somewhere in between dawn and dusk like 5 minutes after a sunset and 5 minutes before a sunrise. Outside the yard and down a black path stood the most beautiful Tipi I have ever seen, inside was an alluring fire and I could see the shapes of men, women turning into strange creatures. I wanted to leave that yard and journey down that path but when I turned around I saw that giant Crow hoping towards me. Then I watched that Raven quickly hop up behind him as arms and hands formed from within his wings and it looked like he was going to grab him. It looked as if they were going to start arguing but instead I watched them get into a fight, black feathers started flying everywhere. The Raven was hitting and choking the Crow who didn't even fight back he just curled up into a ball on the ground. I ran up to them and told something my mother said to me.

"You shouldn't fight each other. You're family and when

times get hard, you're all each other's got." I yelled
The Raven looked at me and said.

"… And what do you know of family boy?" Questioned
the Raven

"I have 4 older brothers who love me and protect me.
But I hate it when they fight and pick on me. I hate it when
anyone fights and picks on me. It makes me feel lonely." I
began to sob, remembering what it feels like to be teased, I
was doing my best trying not to cry.

But those memories and emotions flooded my mind especially
when I looked at that poor nice Crow curled up on the
ground, I started to cry remembering what it feels like. Because
when you pick on someone, you make them feel all alone.
Some people say that's the worst kind of feeling you can have
especially when someone or some people make you feel it.

As the tears ran down my face they hit the ground and the
ground itself shook with every tear drop. When the world
shook something changed within the mean Raven who looked
at me and smiled. He let his grip go of the younger Crow, but
not before saying.

"Tell him what you must, but make sure you show him
the way out. I'd hate for him to get lost out here. Lord knows
he won't ever find his way home certainly not on his own and
he also might get eaten" Explained the Raven who all of a
sudden was not so mean. I watched as his hands and arms
went back into his feathers and became wings once again.

The Crow slowly got up and hopped over towards me.

"Caw Caw CAW?" He asked

"Are you ok?" I said as I wiped the tears away.
The crow bobbed its head up and down.

"Caw Caw CAW?" Questioned the Crow.

"I can't understand you."

"Caw Caw CAW?"

As I began to pet his head the raven hopped over to me and
said.

"You know out here all you have to do is want to
understand and you will."

I looked at the Crow right into his eyes and said

"I really want to understand you."

"Caw…. Caw… I said. What is the last thing you remember?" asked the Crow.

"I don't know, the last thing I remember was watching the sky at night." I Explained

"And what did you see?" Inquired the Crow

"I saw four stars fall down to the earth, they fell further than I could see. Then when they hit the earth I saw a light. And now I'm here." I Answered

The Crow smiled, like magic he grew two arms and then two hands, than 5 yellow balls appeared in his hand out of thin air. He tried to juggle but all the balls fell down. One of those balls bounced right onto my hand and it turned into a chocolate cake, which was my favourite kind of cake. Actually chocolate covered anything is my favourite. Before I started to eat, this is what he said.

"Whoa, hold on a second! That's dream flavoured cake you're about to eat. It is dream food and it's super special. When you eat it, you'll remember this dream. BUT! You'll also remember what I'm about to say." Explained the Crow

He looked at me and laughed.

"Find those stars, learn the secret that each one possesses. Sometimes they'll find you and sometimes you'll find each other." He revealed

He smiled and winked at me, dreams are funny things.

"How do I get out of here? That raven said I might get eaten and I don't want to be anyone's supper."

"Oh it's simple, you just have to close your eyes and remember. But before you go remember this one thing."

"What?"

"On this path beautiful and terrible things will happen. But don't be afraid."

"That's kind of scary."

"That's ok! Because if you ever get into trouble be sure to remember this other one thing. And it will always help you out no matter what."

I watched him open up his mouth but as he spoke but no words came out like someone hit the mute button on him. He might have been speaking but I couldn't hear a word he was saying.

"I can't hear you."

He shook his head almost like he understood what was happening and then motioned to my hand which held the cake. I took a bite and man was that cake delicious I can't explain how to you how delicious it tasted. Everything for a second went black and I could hear the sound of wings as they were flapping. Before I knew it I woke up.

I sat up and my eyes immediately locked onto my window sill, on it was a black feather. Something inside of me had changed, I had just realised something inside me was missing. Like a puzzle you think is complete until you look around and see that a piece is absent. The weird feeling was I felt like it was always missing and I didn't know about it until just then but then I remembered all at once I wasn't whole. I jumped up and looked out of the window scanning out into the horizon to see where the stars fell. I could feel those stars calling out to me as if they had that missing piece.

My mother came into the room and turned on the lights, it was time for school. She was frowning as she looked into my eyes seeing the bags which had formed from a lack of sleep and knew I had stayed up late. Mothers always seemed to catch those things both big and small. But I just had to tell her all about the dream, about the butterfly and the Raven and the Crow and as I did, she sat on my bed looked at me and smiled.

"Sounds like a beautiful dream and it sounds like a special dream, Butterflies carry you into the dream world."

"Do they" I asked

"Yes they're very sacred to us. Do you know who the Raven and Crow are?"

"Ummm, no."

"They're Spirits, especially when you dream of them two together. I don't think I ever told you about who painted all the birds in the animal kingdom."

13

"Nope, I never heard that story"
I walked over to the bed and sat beside her.

"Well, those two birds are very special, very creative and mischievous, but they're always fighting. Ravens are generally bigger which means he tends to bully around his younger brother. Crows tend to be smaller and often they have to rely on their wits. So they fight and trick each other constantly, it happens even today now that you tell about your dream. One day, way back when the world was new, all birds looked alike and had the same colour. These birds had their own tribes and nations and with each nation came with protocol, a way to act. Their protocol is bird songs which are sacred stories and ceremonies. If you listen during certain parts of the day, you can hear those songs. "Napi" gifted an enormous task to the Raven and Crow. They were to paint all the other birds, for the Raven and Crow knew many of the earth's and sky worlds secrets, they knew patterns and they knew paints. There are no 2 other types of birds in the animal kingdom that could do this important task, so each went out and gathered paints and looked at the earth's patterns, both secret and invisible. They knew a job from Napi was a big thing of great importance and they wanted to do their best, so one by one they gathered all the birds of all the bird kingdoms into one place. The painting place. They started painting each bird and only got progressively better and more detailed beautiful with each bird painted. Both the Raven and Crow boasted to each bird as they left, that by the end they were going to have the most beautiful painting job. At last it was finally down to those two. But the Raven bullied the Crow and said paint me as thee most beautiful, for good measure he hit the Crow on the head. The crow started painting and out of anger made the Raven look like an ugly clown. The Raven saw his reflection in one of the paints and charged the Crow and they fought all over the painting place. They crashed into the paint and rolled in other paints and do you know what all colours at once are?"

"...Black?"
My Mother laughed

"Yes, because they couldn't get along they ended up with the most basic and embarrassing painting job. And that's why they look the way they do even today."

"I feel sorry for the Crow, mom he was nice and the Raven was mean to him in my dream."

"I wouldn't feel too bad for him, he's probably tricking the Raven even as we speak. Those two boys never seem to get along... But you got to get up and get ready for school."

I walked over to the window and looked out remembering where the stars fell.

"What do you think is out there? Out in the world?"

"Life"

My Mother smiled, gave me a kiss and left the room, she didn't notice the black feather.

THE BUILDING ROOM

I grabbed that feather and placed it under my pillow. I woozily, drowsily and tiredly carried on throughout the day doing my best to stay awake in school. I found myself looking out the window losing interest in whatever the teacher was saying and kept thinking about how the sky lit up when the stars landed.

The day passed quickly and I was home and walked to my room so incredibly exhausted. As I opened the door the room itself was pitch black unusual for this time of day. I closed the door behind me and turned on the lights.

The room lit up for a brief second I realised I was no longer in my room. I was in a place that was surrounded by darkness except for a single light that hung over a concrete bed. I walked up to it examining the structure there were these strange and beautiful markings engraved all over. I began to trace those markings with my fingers tips feeling the cool smooth divots in the bed of concrete.

"HAHA!" I heard a man laughing.

Startled I turned around and seen an old man with dark brown wrinkly skin and long greying hair walking towards me. I didn't feel scared by this man's presence. Something about him seemed familiar.

"It is a funny thing indeed meeting you here. I was

wondering when you would show up."

"Where am I? And who are you?" I asked

"You are in the building room. At least that's what I was told when I was your age. Who am I? One day you might find out. We don't have much time to talk about you or me. I have a really, really long history that we can't quite get into just yet. In fact we don't have much time at all"

"Time for what?"

"We don't have much time for you being here. You're going to be taken from this place very quickly. No one of your age is allowed to be in the building room for too long."

"I don't understand."

"No I suppose you don't. I didn't either when I was your age. How old are you again?"

"I'm"

"Actually that doesn't really matter either, I know you were given something special recently. Do you have it?"

"I was given a toy train for my birthday."

"No, not from the waking world from the dream world."

"Oooh! I have a feather but it's under my pillow."

"Silly boy, when you're given something it will always be with you. Try reaching into your pocket."

I reached into my pocket and felt the steam of the feather. I pulled slowly as to not ruffle the threads. Slowly it came out of my pocket.

"OK! GREAT! Black, WOW! what a beautiful color. Now place that feather onto **The Corpus**. The concrete slab"

I did as I was instructed. A blinding light emitted from the table. I shielded my eyes until the flash passed and when it did I looked back on the table.

I could see an outline that it kind of looked like the skin of a jelly fish. It was hollow and nothing was inside but the outline had a form and it changed and then changed again. I touched it but my hand went right through the object it was both warm and cold at the same time.

"What just happened?"

"Something incredible! You did quite well actually!"

"Where's my feather?"

"Doing its job right now. All feathers are sacred but it's become something more than just a feather on top of the Corpus!"

"A Corpus? ...But"

"Sorry no time for questions."

"Yeah, but"

"No time for that either."

He walked me to the door and opened it.

"You will see me again. I promise. Every time you collect something special come see me. But for now you must wake."

He pushed me through.

I was back in my room lying on the floor. I must have fallen asleep as soon as I got in. I jumped up and quickly looked under the pillow for my feather. I saw nothing. I wanted to be upset but that old man's words came back again. When you're given something it will always be with you.

ONE OF THE FOUR

Enjoy your youth because time flies rapidly especially when you're young and it flies even faster when you're having fun. We as a family moved way up north to be with my Fathers' (your Grandfathers') people 'The Dene'. The Dene people live far, far away from 'The Blackfoot' rez I grew up on. Our new home was in a small city that was surrounded by the boreal forest, it had trees and plants that stretched out for hundreds of miles as far as the eye could see. People in this small city seemed to live, work and die in this little corner of the world. Much like my little rez, people had the idea they were always going to be there and if they believed in it enough they usually proved themselves right. It is a strange thing to look back at your childhood because the years just seem to fall off the calendar like seconds. In what felt like a flash I was no longer a young boy I had grown into a young man.

One of my regrets is that I wish I had spent more time with my father growing up but never did. He was always too busy working and too busy with life. I remember the little things that we did together and those little things always meant the world to me. He would take me into the bush and we would hike for hours. I was happiest out in the wilderness walking amongst the trees, the rivers and creeks.

My father took me on these long wilderness expeditions showing me what he knew; making fires, talking about some medicines and explaining little mysteries of creation that surrounded us. Right before my eyes he just cut off a branch from a red willow and carved and fashioned a whistle and boy it sounded amazing. I loved our time in the wilderness although he seldom took me for walks. It was one of those gifts we simply do not get enough of as a child or one of those amazing things we take for granted. The bush became my second home and I never truly felt free unless I was out in the wilderness.

As time went on he took me out less and less but I still hiked with or without him. I was always careful not to venture too far out in case I got hurt or got lost. A lot of things can happen out in the bush some of these things have rationale explanations and others fall into the realm of the unbelievable. You have to be careful because you never know which one side you'll find yourself in.

I stood on the edge of a tree line with my pack I had rain gear, a sweater, matches and water. It was always good to be prepared but something's you can never really prepare for. This day was different maybe it was in the air or maybe it was me, either way I could not wait to get out onto the land. I was all smiles entering the wilderness welcoming the change from the city to the earth. Even though I usually ventured on an internal safe boarder today I had this feeling inside, a calling to go further and further out into the wild. Every time I wanted to turn around something drew me out. I found a small stream that turned into a water fall, I sat by it for a little while listening to the rhythm and sound of falling water.

The bush is a wonderful place to be, it is said that 'All life's creation starts at the rivers, streams and lakes'. You can always find the most amount of plant life near the water and there's way too many different kinds of plants for me to name or even count. Plants have families just like you although they are just a little different, they are still a very close family. Even though we cannot always see it, the bush is so incredibly connected.

The animals roam free, running, hunting, hiding and living. There is so much beauty in that world. It's the reason why I love to hike, I love to walk and I love to explore the bush, sometimes by myself and sometimes with my friends.

I was hiking and on my way back but was still a few hours and still quite a few miles away from home. On this particular day, I lost track of time as night was falling faster than I had expected. Most times when I was hiking I wasn't afraid. Nights however, did freak me out because everything that's beautiful during the day becomes deeply frightening in the darkness, plus you hear really spooky sounds. I would create the creepiest ghouls and picture the biggest of beasts stalking me. My mind would always seem to invent fantastic new terrors, each scarier than the last. Giant wolves, taller than the tallest trees with huge razor sharp teeth that were constantly hungry for fresh human blood or bears with enormous claws and paws that could easily wrap around a body and in one gulp swallow you whole. I was walking trying to forget those things that take home in the darkest of places and get home in one piece.

The wind began to pick up as the last bits of sunlight fell into the night sky. I knew I shouldn't have went out as far as I did into the bush and now I would definitely be walking home in the dark. Something jumped out of focus in the corner of my eye I immediately looked around scanning the horizon. Instead of walking towards home where I should have been I was more interested in finding whatever it was. I remember being equal parts scared and equal parts excited. I had seen something flicker off in the distance on top of a hill. I didn't know if this something was shiny or glowing or sparkly. But I had to find out so I walked towards that something.

Each step brought me closer to this hill, and it was no ordinary hill. I had hiked this area many times over and not once did I ever see it before. The hill was large and it shot up out of place in the middle of a valley. At the base of the hill there were trees that were tall, thick and old, there was green moss that wrapped and encased the trees. These trees tightly circled the hill almost like a barrier or maybe as soldiers standing as protectors. Beyond the trees the hill itself was barren with one black path leading up and at the top there was a mysterious light slowly blinking. I looked up and saw a very steep climb. The air around me suddenly became cold and moist I couldn't tell if it was because the sun had finally set or if it was because I was so close to this hill. I took a deep breath in and as I exhaled I could see my breath leave my mouth. So I reached into my backpack and pulled out and put on a sweater. I stared at the light entranced and enchanted and also very puzzled at what that light actually was. It was almost like it was calling out my name. I had to see it, I had to figure out what it was. I had to know its secret so I began to climb. The further up the hill I got the brighter it seemed to get. The wind picked up violently making a howling sound as it passed through the trees. I could feel the fear building as dust, earth and leaves kicked up from the ground and blew to the heavens.

When I came within a foot of that light the wind stopped blowing. I looked around and saw that everything stopped, like time itself froze. Particles of dust and leaves were suspended in mid-air. I was in complete awe looking around at the world as time stood still. I plucked a leaf from the air it was cold to touch I let it go almost immediately expecting it to drop to the ground but it remained in the air suspended. I grabbed another leaf and crushed it. When I opened my hand I could see the pieces broken apart and they remained exactly as it was fragmented in the air. I couldn't help but smile at the odd peculiarity I was experiencing.

Then I heard a sound emitting from the light. It was a quiet ringing that began to reverberate transforming into a low comfortable hum. I looked down at the ground and saw the light the closer I got, the more I felt something. It was blinding as it was beautiful to behold. I reached down to pick it up and had to close my eyes from its intensity. Against my will acting on its own my body instantly took in a deep breath.

Within this moment the light had revealed a secret to me, the secret of always feeling at home. It said to look within my heart, that my heart was and always will be my home. Take care of your heart and you'll take care of your home. From then on, no matter where I was or how far I went. I would never get homesick, I would always feel my heart, my home.

...I had found the first star

Yet I still felt like a piece of me was missing.

MOUNTAINS AND THE MEDICINE MAN

It's really hard to talk about finding a star, most people get lost in the explanation. Some people will look at you like you were crazy, incoherent and others would tell you that you just had a very nice dream. After a while I decided not to tell anyone about it.

When I was growing up, sometimes I had a lot of friends and sometimes it seemed like I had no friends at all. I was lost, confused and angry at the world around me, why did a piece of me feel like it was missing? I was mad because I couldn't find any answers to the questions I had about my life. I had no direction and some people I was friends with seemed to have everything figured out. I was one of those people that didn't.

That's when I first began travelling. I had just graduated from high school and like everyone else around me, I was beginning to buy into the idea that I was going to spend the rest of my life up North. I didn't want that but I could feel my life shifting in that direction. It was just like the dream I had as a kid being tied down in a room that was burning down around me. So, I took the first chance presented to me to get out of the city I took it to see what the world had to offer.

I joined a program with all different Indigenous youth from around Canada. We had to live in the wilderness of the Rocky

Mountains in tipi's. Every day we gathered water from a mountain stream and cooked all our meals over a fire. Every day we hauled water from the creek to drink and even bathed in that ice cold mountain water. The kind of cold that when it hits your body it pushes the air uncontrollably out of your lungs and back out into the atmosphere. Yet when you drink it for the first time nothing tastes as pure and as clean. It's a medicine and something to completely revivify the soul.

We we're also learning how to hike through the mountains as on any given day you can experience all four seasons spring, summer, fall and winter. The mountains are amazing and also dangerous. We were planning to go on an 8 day back packing trip with just the food and clothing we could carry on our backs. I had set up my gear bag thinking it was way too heavy. Our wilderness guide saw me struggling and said laughing "In a few days it'll get lighter and then you'll realise we're running out of food. Take pleasure in the weight you carry it will help to sustain you." Before we all began to head out he bode a forewarning "Also pray we don't get caught up in a blizzard that lasts for days cause we could get stuck god knows where for god knows how long."

Daybreak hit and we left, if you have never seen the sunlight on the mountains at first light, let me tell you it's something incredible. Everything is dark grey and almost devoid of all colour, the world is so quiet and it's like the wind doesn't even want to blow. All at once the sunrays creep down the tips of the mountain tops bringing colour as it paints the world anew again. It only lasts for brief seconds to see everything around you change from grey and black into a colourful collection of beauty. Get up early enough and you can see the natural world wake.

With our bags packed we left, crossing rivers, creeks, streams and the ever changing landscape. The soil must have been less than a few inches deep if you step to hard you hit the rock of the mountains but it was deep enough to grant life a chance. There was an abundant amount of plant species around us. We moved through pass ways and clearings between the narrow ways found at the bottom of two mountains almost growing together or it was like that had split into two ages ago. I never thought you could walk through the past and yet here we were retracing the pathways of our ancestors.

During our trip we had hard days, I remember how sore our legs and feet were. But each day we went we were rewarded with the most beautiful landscape. Sometimes when we walked we over looked into a valley and other days we were in a valley. The pain of climbing was worth the visual reward.

Days passed on quicker than the next and our packs got a bit easier to carry. I think it was the combination of our growing strength and our decreasing food supply. We moved through the select and best meals first and saving what we deemed the most undesirable thing to consume which was a big bag called 'Spaghetti Tofu'. In the beginning we took a vote and it was unanimous, nobody in our group wanted to eat it. With each day passing it brought us closer to that dreaded last meal.

I've always had a fondness for looking at maps, trying to discover shortcuts or create more efficient paths. Looking back now I must have studied that map every night before sleep carefully calculating how long it would take for us to get back to the city. We were a little more than half way when the weather began to change for the worse.

That morning I'll never forget, we were in a narrow passageway on an island with creeks ankle deep that ran swift but quiet which created an interesting water harmony, natures natural lullaby. The mountains rose on either side us stretching up into the havens just passed the clouds. To the east you could see the sunrise over a clear blue sky, but the more westward you get, the more clouds began to funnel in creating a dome of grey. I looked up and saw the grey of the clouds slowly began to crawl down the mountain sides breaking off into little streams one by one before the rest followed suit. It was phenomenal.

Our guide woke up and saw the same thing but instead of a look of wonderment he had one of worry. Then he turned his gaze to us and told us all to get ready that we needed to move out soon, we had 10 – 12 km to cover today and with any luck it wouldn't blizzard. If it did blizzard as we were hiking we would be in a spot of trouble but we would be worse off and in dire straits if we stayed where we were and got caught in heavy snow fall.

We broke camp and started walking the whole trip up until this point was mildly warm now with the absence of the sun it began to steadily get colder. Mid-day we stopped for a brief lunch, which was simply tea and assorted nuts. The weather was making the day miserable everywhere we walked was cold, damp and wet. Even the gear we carried and the clothes we wore became soaked and tattered.

There was an overcast that was just above the mountains and it felt like a rain storm was closing in. Then the wind began to blow hard and fast, we had to make cover under a ridge as rocks were being blown off the side of the mountains. The wind began to tear through the narrow ways between the mountain side crying out loud whistles and screams. I could feel fear growing inside that this would never stop and never end. That we would be stuck here cold and miserable, forever.

Then all at once everything stopped and we ventured out of the ridge back into the pass. The immediate overcast had blown away and as we looked up we could see another overcast much higher in the sky still blocking out the sun. Our guide had a look of panic.

"We need to make camp and we also need a supplies list of how much food we have remaining."

"Why?" I asked

"A blizzards moving in. And I don't know how many days we will be pinned down here."

"Can we hike out of here?"

"No we got too many miles to cover. It'll be a complete white out and it's way too dangerous to try. We're going to have to buckle down and wait out the storm."

"How long will that take?"

"Hopefully not before our food runs out."

We quickly got into a pass near some trees and began to

make camp. I was trying not to be scared as I was scanning the map. If we marched full speed it would take the rest of today and most of tomorrow for us to come out of the wilderness. It would be long hard days but possible. The snow began to fall it was thick white flakes that began to melt the second they hit the ground. After a while a blanket of snow began to coat the floor. As we set up out tents they began to fall in greater numbers and faster. It was in the nick of time too because just as we had our tents up the snow fell so hard that you couldn't see a foot in front of your eyes. At the centre of our camp was our guide who had built and lit a great fire. The fire helped to improve our visibility we could see where our tents where. The temperature dropped again and we found ourselves walking to and warming ourselves by the blaze.

As the sun set and the world darkened everything that was wet began to freeze and the temperature was still rapidly dropping. But that wasn't the thing freaking us out, we came upon our last meal 'Spaghetti Tofu". Tofu can taste great if you know how to prepare it, but none of us knew how to prep it. We tried our best as we cooked it over the fire. It was probably the foulest thing I have ever eaten. It tasted awful in the mouth but when it hits the stomach, my stomach wanted no part of it and kept trying to reject it anyway possible. The sad painful truth that we all did share in was the fact that we would have to ration this meal for the next couple of days. We finished our meals quietly.

Our guide was beginning to tell us a story of creation but also how in almost all creation stories they all begin with the darkness. The void, the emptiness, the nothing and how in all these stories the light was born within the darkness. All things he said took shape and were created from the darkness. It wasn't a thing to be afraid of because you never quite know what the darkness will gift you.

In the middle of his story we heard a huge crash like a tree that had suddenly fallen over. He stopped for a second and looked out into the distance he was scanning for something or someone. I looked and looked and I couldn't see anything outside of the fire he built. There was a thick wall of snow that was falling and beyond that was the night.

"Do you see something?"

"Not quite"

A moment later a smile grew on his face.

"You're in for quite a treat."

"Why?"

"I was wondering if he would show."

"Who?"

A moment later a black silhouette appeared walking towards the fire the closer it got the more of it revealed itself. There was a tall man who was bundled up in outdoor gear suited for just this kind of the weather his face was mostly covered by a mask but you could see his eyebrows were thick white and frosted. As he removed the mask from his face he had deep rigged lines and wrinkles, the sign of age. As he pulled off his hood we could see long white flowing hair. I thought he had gloves on but they were covered in what looked like thick black oil. He immediately walked over to the fire and placed his hands into it like he was washing the black sludge off. We all fell silent watching this man. Whatever it was fell from his hands and as the flames touched it a hissing sound was made. When the ooze was completely off he pulled his hands from the fire. Not a burn on them, he should have had some heat trauma, some blistering but nothing. He was smiling looking at his hands and leaned forward and spoke to the fire.

"Thank you." He had spoken and his voice was deep and resounded with power

"What the hell was that?" I asked

"Definitely not from hell. It was a zero."

"A what?"

"A zero. Part of a bigger whole, but this part was terribly cold. I brought it back to the fire so it could warm itself"

"Why?"

"You wouldn't and shouldn't ask a person in distress why they need help, do you? Sometimes it is just best to give without thinking."

"Who are you?"

"Who am I? I'm hungry is what I am. I feel almost famished walking through this white out. What do you have here?"

I had forgotten my manners in what we had just witnessed. He was an elder that travelled through the storm and was hungry. I couldn't help but think back to my Mother and what she would say in my recent actions. *'I raised you better than that'* she'd say.

"Spaghetti Tofu but its tastes terrible. I'm sorry to be so rude, please have a seat. I'll make you a plate."

"Tastes terrible? Terrible, now that's judgement. It's something we have to work hard to remove from our lives. I wouldn't say terrible."

I quickly made him a plate and he took a big smell. I could hear him say Mmmm and then he took a bite. I was expecting him to spit it all out, but his face lit up in joy.

"It's not terrible at all it is just a different kind of delicious."

Our guide leaned over to me and whispered.

"He's a vegetarian."

He ate forkful after forkful until his bowl was completely barren. We all looked in disbelief we didn't know what was more farfetched the fact that he cleaned his hands with fire or that he polished off a full bowl of that repugnant dish.

"Hmmm, That was a different kind of delicious. But thank you, I enjoyed it thoroughly."

I looked out at into the storm and the complete white out and realised we were in the middle of nowhere.

"Where did you come from?"

"That way." He pointed

"You came from the east?"

"Yeah I was. But I took a few short cuts here and there to bring me to this fire"

"Short cuts?" I remembered as I looked at the map there was no short cuts to get to where we were from the east. "I don't remember seeing any kind of shortcuts on the map"

"Not on one of those maps people draw. There are shortcuts and pathways between worlds"

"Between worlds?" It sounded really farfetched but he did wash his hands with fire. The idea of worlds had gotten me thinking "How many worlds are there?"

"About as many as you can think of."

"And you know these pathways that connect worlds."

"Not all of them but I was shown a few and stumbled upon a few others. But that doesn't matter I was saying something before. Now what was it again, oh yeah judgement."

"What about judgement?"

"We have to remove that word from our hearts. If you look at all the world's conflicts and wars at the centre of all of that is judgement. It's the root cause of unnecessary pain and suffering."

"How do we do that, let go of judgement?"

"Learn to love without conditions. To enter into any situation and give thanks, peace and love. The world now so desperately needs a mirror of unconditional love. The world needs you."

I didn't know what to say or what to ask at that moment.

"We're stuck here until the storm lets up. So better make yourself comfortable." Our guide had said to the old man.

"Is that so? Well have you tried talking to it?"

"Talking to what?" I asked

"The weather."

"No. You can do that?"

"You can do whatever you want to. I'll think I'll go and have a conversation with the weather. See if I can get it to change its mind."

"You're going to tell the weather to stop making a blizzard."

"Goodness no, you can't tell the weather anything. It does what it wants. I've only heard of weather changers never met one in person and in these parts there hasn't been one for ages."

31

And just like that he got up as he was leaving I stopped him.

"I never got your name."

"Names, those are important things. They tell you who you are and what your job is in this world or at least they remind you."

"So what's your name?"

"Sequoyah."

"Like the tree?"

"Among a great many other things. But it is only one of my names."

"What are your others?"

"I'll tell you when I come back. I need to converse with this weather." Sequoyah looked around and spoke as if he was talking to not only to me but himself "If I come back if… it permits me to return."

"Ok. Well good luck."

And with that he left.

TWO OF THE FOUR

The bunch of us didn't quite know what to make of it or what to do. We were each left speechless and one by one we said good night and found our way to our tents. I decided to sit by the fire until his return. I kept stoking the flames to keep it blazing so he would have something that would help to navigate his way back.

The minutes turned to hours and still nothing. The storm itself seemed to intensify, I looked around scanning the area trying to find him.

"I don't suppose the conversation went well." I said to myself.

"And what makes you say that?" Sequoyah asked

I was startled I didn't even hear him creep up behind me

"It's snowing harder now."

"Well… to persuade weather to change is not an easy task."

"What did the weather say?"

"It would leave the decision until the morning."

I kept feeling that Sequoyah was a wizard or medicine man.

"Are you a medicine man… or wizard?"

He laughed a deep laugh.

"Hahaha. What makes you say that?"

"The things you say and do, you also have a bit of wizard vibe going on."

"Nah, I am no such thing. I'm just a man that's listening to and guided by spirit. Although one time a little while ago I was run out of a small town because they thought I was a wizard."

"Really?"

"Yeah, but I was reminded of something tonight."

"What was that?"

"A message I was told to give to you."

"Really? Who's it from?"

"It was from what seems like a life time ago. I can't remember who or what it was from. I just know it's for you"

"What's the message?"

"All the pain in your life will bring about understanding, if you accept it."

"Accept what?"

"Your pain."

"And what will happen to my pain once I accept it? Where will it go?"

"Once you embrace it you'll understand it and the creator will take it away."

"I saw something once when I was a child. Ever since then I feel like there's a piece of me missing. I would look for it but I don't know where to go." I explained

"It's ok to be scared and angry with life and the world especially when you feel lost. We're raised too much in that world of the intellect that we forget the basics of all life."

"What's that?"

"Trust in Spirit. It will never misguide or misdirect you. It will always take you where you are supposed to be."

"Hmm..." I felt like I could ask him anything and he would have answer for me "So, what's the trick to life?"

"Trick? There's no trick to make any of it easier. You just have to give thanks."

"Thanks?"

"Yes just say, Thank you. Everything else after that is a

reminder of what you're thankful for."

I sat and looked at the fire for a moment and then back at him.

"Trust in Spirit?"

He smiled like a mentor in appreciation of a lesson passed on.

"Yes."

Then all at once he began to light up so bright that I was blinded. I felt myself falling asleep and could only quickly look around and see the world frozen in time. I heard a rhythmic slow beat, it was like hearing a deep base matching the rhythm of a heartbeat. Maybe it was a heartbeat of the fire I was hearing or maybe it was Sequoyah's heartbeat. The flames held their dance and became motionless, the snowflakes froze completely still in air, the breath that left my mouth stayed perfectly suspended. Nothing was moving but Sequoyah as he smiled, looking around and laughing.

You ever have that moment when someone turns the lights on as your sleeping. Everything becomes bright white as your eyes begin to adjust. That's what was happening. A moment later I was being shook awake by our guide. I looked around and was by the fire place somehow in my sleeping bag. I could see the sky it was a beautiful ocean blue and the sun was shining. The storm and blizzard had passed.

"Get up! You've slept most of the morning away."

"Where's Sequoyah?"

"He must have left throughout the night."

"Where did he go?"

"I don't know. Somewhere out there."

"Where is he from?"

"I don't know, somewhere out east."

"What does his name mean, Sequoyah?"

"Haha. It means Pigs Legs. He likes it, says it keeps him humble."

"Pigs Legs."

"Yeah. But he's gifted names in his travels from people all over and they all usually translate into the same thing."

"What's that?"

"The Light."

35

"Hmmm."

"But I liked one translation this one group of people from the south called him."

"What was it?"

"It was light, but it was the Star light. The kind of light you see it when it shoots across the night sky."

You couldn't wipe that smile off my face not for the rest of the trip. Our packs were lighter and each step brought us closer to our final destination. The weather was incredible it wasn't too warm nor too cold and if it did get hot a nice refreshing wind always seem to blow by. I think our speed doubled in our enthusiasm as we were covering more ground than we ever had. I was looking back every few steps half expecting to see Sequoyah behind us. He wasn't and I knew deep down inside he wouldn't be. That night we ate the final portion of our 'Spaghetti Tofu' we all dreaded that last meal. Before I ate my first forkful I smelled it and said "Thank you". Thinking to myself that it was a different kind of delicious hoping that mindset would magically change the taste. The meal was still the most terrible thing I ever ate but I was just glad we were done with it, hopefully I would never have to eat something so grotesque.

Before we knew it our hike through the mountains was finished. I looked back one last time to the temporary place I called home. I remembered what Sequoyah told me, to trust in Spirit.

..I had found the second star

Yet I still felt like a piece of me was missing.

THE BUILDING ROOM

Have you ever been to a place you remember fondly? And then when you go back it's not as big or as amazing as you remember? You slide down a hill during winter and are awe struck at its immensity and then you return it's not nearly as big. Places and faces do that from time to time. I had almost forgotten about 'The Building Room' in fact I could vaguely remember that place. It was a beautiful dream I had as a child and the older I had gotten the less sense it made.

But there I was in a concrete room and everything was pitch black except for the place in the middle. I could see a formless thing changing shapes and that odd old man looking at it. The place itself didn't change in fact it looked bigger than I remember. I slowly walked forwards.

"... um excuse me."

The old man turned around.

"Goodness you gave me quite a startle. And you're back so soon but my how you've aged."

"Soon? Aged? I haven't been here in like 10 years"

"Hmm. Well I guess perception of time is a lot different in this place... or maybe it's my perception of time that's off."

"Have you been here all this time?"

"My dear boy what did I just say? I literally just pushed

you out that door and walked back over here when you came creeping up on me."

"Seriously?"

"Yes, but where are we again? You must have something for me a gift and by the looks of it two gifts. Oh gosh I wish it was my birthday."

"I found two stars. But I don't know how to give them to you or what you're going to do with them."

"Hmm well the easiest way is for you to just close your eyes, hold out your hands and tell me about the stars."

"Tell you about them?"

"Yeah. Tell me their secret."

I looked at him long and hard for a moment, there was something about him that I could just immediately trust. He felt very familiar almost like he was… family. I closed my eyes held out my hands and took a deep breath in.

"When I found the first star the one thing I can remember was to make my heart my home."

"Ha! Great now open your eyes."

I opened them and within my hands was a burning star. It was like a ball of warm golden light, it felt very comfortable to hold. Star Dust fell frequently like holding those hand held sparklers and the flames dissolving before they ever touched the ground. I was lost looking at it.

"Now quickly place it near on the corpus next to the shapeless thing."

"The corpus?" I said as I placed the star next one the shapeless thing. We watched as it slowly absorbed the star, it had colors and would change frequently.

The old man looked around quickly.

"Oh goodness, were running out of time again. Hurry tell me about the other star." I could feel his anxiety.

I closed my eyes and held out my hands.

"Trust in Spirit."

I opened my eyes again and the stars was burning bright, so bright I had to squint. I walked over to the corpus and placed the star down. This time the thing wasted no time absorbing it.

Along with changing colours it seemed to be able to hold and change numerous shapes. Most people would say it looked strange but I thought it looked beautiful.

"What's going on?"

"Oh I can't tell you right now without explaining everything and that will take a very, very long time."

Again he was walking me to the door very quickly.

"Well what can you tell me?"

"You're doing a magnificent job. Just remember to bring me the things you collect and we can continue. Hurry back. There isn't much time!"

And just like that he pushed me through the door again.

A STRANGE YET BEAUTIFUL WORLD

The first time I was in love it was all things at once; astonishing, breathtaking and horrible. Absolutely horrible, the horrible part is of course at the end which we call heart break. But everything up until that moment is amazing and surreal you can't even begin to define or explain it. You enter into a kind of craze, but it's a good kind crazy and one hell of a ride, so enjoy it. Some men and women never recover once the ride is over. I won't get into all the mushy details of how I fell in love. I will tell you how I got through my first heart break. And please don't ask me for her name because I just won't' tell you.

I was young and in love but you already knew that but what you might not know is that no matter where I went she was always on my mind. I left and traveled around, seeing different parts of Canada, the mountains, the plains, the oceans and all the land in between. But my thoughts would always come back to her. Things weren't working out, we wanted different things and we're becoming different people. It happens and that's life. We all go through it. Remember that pride often gives way to regret and you can either wallow in it or explore what lay ahead.

Everywhere I went and every expression I seen of beauty both natural and manmade, I saw her face, her eyes, her everything. When you're in love it's the most amazing feeling but when you're out of favour with love it is agonizing. It can drive a sane person crazy and not the good kind of crazy mind you. Being lost in that dark place of a broken heart sometimes you just need to get out for a bit. That's what I did. I had seen so much of this land yet everything reminded me of her. I decided enough was enough and I was going to go someplace I had never been. There was a program that offered people a chance to work with youth in the jungles of South America. It was a little country just south of the Caribbean ocean called Guyana. I signed up, who wouldn't jump at the chance to see the world?

I remember the plane taking off. It happens just like that, you don't really know about an adventure you wander into but there I was on a plane as the tires left the tarmac. My stomach felt a bit wheezy and that's always a great feeling to have when starting an adventure. It felt like all of this was happening suddenly and all too quickly, the jungle as I'm told can be a very dangerous place.

Thoughts began to run through my mind, would I ever see home again? I placed my hand to my heart and remembered back to what the star had shared with me.

You know the way the world feels when you're at home, it always feels the same no matter what. It's a constant beautiful feeling.

Well the way it is when you leave on an airplane for the first time you leave all that comfort in the unchanged and then as you land the world transforms and the unchanged quickly becomes the exotic. And you're in it, something new.

The doors to the plane opened and the heat and humidity hit. It was hot, hotter than the hottest day I have ever experienced. The kind of heat where even if you sit down in the shade doing nothing you still sweat buckets. I got off the plane and walked upon a foreign soil and nothing seemed the same. Thinking to myself within my family I knew of no one in my ancestral line that has ever treaded these lands. It's a really cool

41

feeling to have, to be the first one.

Guyana is a poorer country that had some rich areas and houses. The first thing I noticed was that everyone was brown or black I hardly seen any white people. The second thing I noticed was that I was about a foot taller than everybody else. I've always been a big person but down there I might have been one of the tallest men in the country.

I collected my bags and was escorted to a bus. The drive would take an estimated 13 hours from the coast to the plains nearing the jungle. There was only one major road heading south and for the most part it was unpaved. It was bumpy and downright treacherous, any man might have quit while he was ahead but I was trusting in spirit. It guided me here how much further was it going to take me?

I hardly slept a wink on what seemed like the longest bus ride of my life, sometimes we hit a slight bump other times we bounced all over the road. I think our driver might have lost control a few times. But we eventually made it. We left the cities on the coast drove through the plains till we reached the edges of the outer jungle. There was no electricity, no running water and not a vehicle anywhere in sight after the bus pulled away. I walked over to where the camp was, the walk was a few kilometers long. It felt like I just stepped way back in time.

I was unpacking my bag when this woman came over, she was about my age. I thought she was interested in me because I was from a different place. She said that I came from strange lands to the north. In her hand she had a gift, two pieces of fruit. They looked like oranges but were green. I asked

"What are those?"

"Green oranges"

"Green… oranges?"

"Yeah, there oranges but green." She said with a weird look on her face, like she was imparting the most common knowledge.

I thought to myself, we call them oranges because they're the colour orange. But these ones were green, what if we found these ones first would we call them greens instead of oranges?

They looked unripe to eat, I said thank you and placed the fruit into my pocket. She laughed at me.

"You have weird manners."

"Why?"

"Because out here when someone gives you food or drink it's time for a visit."

"A visit?"

"Yes where we share stories, I want to hear about what it is like where you come from."

I had told her a bit about what life was like as I peeled the green orange. How the cities were made of concrete and some buildings stretched into the sky. How other cities were so big that when you climbed up those buildings you could see the city stretch far out into the horizon. I took a bite of the green orange, it tasted so incredibly sweet. I told her that white people were in abundance where I was from. If you got sick you could call and an ambulance would be near you within 8 minutes. I wanted to tell her more, but she simply said thank you and walked away.

That first night after sunset, I was treated with one of the jungles many gifts. Howler monkeys. They sleep in packs of 15 to 20 and each has its own distinct voice. One or two usually stay up and watch each other's back. Then at the sound or feeling of something dangerous, they begin to shout to wake each other up. When one hears a scream they all start up and don't stop till all 15 to 20 have woken up. Then just like that they run away and their sounds fade into the jungle. It's the oddest thing you'll ever hear.

They housed me in a hut, it was made of wood and leaves. The doorways were pretty small, every time I entered and exited a house I had to duck. I was sleeping in a hammock because it was the best defense against bugs and insects. Those Guyanese people knew how to make a great shelter as it kept out the torrential rains and held up against some pretty windy days. It was awesome I loved when a gentle or strong wind would blow by because they always carried such a unique scent.

The smell of the jungle was a mixture and multitude of different plant species. From the sky looking down, the bush was thick and close together like giant tree broccoli. When you where on the ground you could see millions of plants. There was so many and it is weird to say but it actually smelled green, I loved it. The sounds of the jungle had something new for every hour moving into the night and back into morning. It's never quiet and something you would think came from an animal had actually come from a reptile or an insect or something else. The sounds would often amalgamate and fuse together creating their own ever-changing jungle language. The heat always knocked me out during the mid-afternoon and when it rained, it poured hard. The raindrops were huge and warm and never let up for hours. You could see a thick white fog coming in from the distance, a wall of rain that came rushing in. When it did everything was given a beautiful refreshing drink. The animals were a lot smaller than back home but the insects and everything else was a lot bigger. It seemed like almost everything was poisonous down there. You would see one type of reptile or insect and there was another that looked almost like it and that, if bitten, licked or rubbed up against you, would kill you and it would be in the most painful manner. Those things were everywhere, every morning that I had gotten up I'd shake out my boots and all kinds of creepy crawly life forms fell to the ground and ran away. The villages were housed with huts and the huts were made of wood and leaves. I had to be careful not to get hurt or be poisoned because if I did and it was serious there was no hospitals not for at least a 100 miles in every direction.

The people of the jungle had their own unique magic that felt so close home. I saw so many parallels between the way they live and the way we live on the rez. They had rez dogs, the hounds that roamed in packs that people fed and were always looking for food here and there. But I did notice something quite peculiar about those dogs, they groomed each other. I'm not kidding I sat down and watched them pick and bite the fleas off of each other. One by one they each took turns.

Everyone took care of one another even the animals like they were all extended family. Aunties weren't aunties they were treated and respected as if they were your other mother. Cousins who were close in age were siblings. As for birthdays everyone showed up some to eat, others to drink but everyone was together. And they were so musical singing songs, humming harmonies and often times creating songs on the spot. I was thinking that I might just spend the rest of my life down there, if it wasn't for the next couple things that happened.

I was housed near a community school they sent in a whole lot of youth from the surrounding villages. Some children were so far away from home they had to stay there throughout the whole year. It reminded me of the past and our people. How your grandparents and ancestors were forced into some bad schools, where they had to stay for a long time. During their lunch break and after school I would play games with a lot of these students. We played traditional Indigenous games, European games, Guyanese games and even created games. It reminded me a lot of playing with my nephews and nieces from back home. We all just clicked and everyday they would come by and we'd hang out.

Each night my friend would come by always with some different kind of fruit and she'd ask me questions about back home. She didn't care too much about the cities and loved hearing about the Rez and how life was so similar. Once she felt the conversation was done she'd always say thank you and then leave.

Life was beautiful down there you would forget even for a moment that you were completely unplugged from electricity and most modern innovations. No computers, no I-pods, no Television. It made you appreciate the world around especially being in between the jungle and the plains. There was so many things you'd miss if you were to just walk around without a care in the world, when you stopped and looked at the ground especially in the jungle you could see the movement of insects that seemed to make the ground come alive. But you needed to watch with the right kind of eyes.

The sun looked huge when it began to set which was every day at 6 pm and it would rise each day at 6 am. The sunset were, well there is no word in the English language that could explain the nature and the beauty of it all. Every day at dusk as the sun would slowly begin its descent over the horizon. It always passed by this mountain in the distance and the mountain itself stood alone out in the prairies. The locals told me that jaguars gathered at the mountain to watch the sunset and that during the day it was a place to gather medicines for all kinds of ailments but at night it transformed and travelers met certain death.

You always had to have one eye peeled and constantly on guard you never knew of the insects and reptiles that were poisonous. But not just the insects and reptiles some plants could kill you if you ate them, others like razor grass cut you sharp and deep if you brushed up against its edge.

The jungle is so beautiful and dangerous.

MONKEYS AND SNAKES

One morning I woke to howler monkeys, it was just before sunrise. They couldn't have been more than a five minute walk away from where I slept. I was told to stay near the edges of the jungle. For all the dangers which just seemed to grow the further you walked in. But these were monkeys... MONKEYS.

I walked into the jungle carefully at first looking at my feet and watching my every step you never quite knew where something poisonous was crawling around. A moment before the howlers were screaming and shouting as I entered the noise all but died down. And for a second the jungle was silent, which it never was.

I let out a sigh thinking that I would never see any real live wild monkeys. Let down I turned around and starting walking back to my hut. Then I felt something hit me hard in the head. I rubbed the ache on my head and seen a grey stick hit the ground. I looked up and seen a group of Howler monkeys sitting up in the trees. They must have gotten curious to see a human walking around and fell silent when I ran into the jungle.

"That kind of hurt you know." I said still rubbing my head.

They sat there silently looking at me and looking at each other. I gazed up and couldn't believe I was seeing real live monkeys. They didn't say anything but they looked like they were up to something. They gave each other a few glances and half hiding smiles, it was like they were on the verge of laughter. Then all at once they threw a bunch of things they had in their hands. Some was food, some was sticks and some was rocks. I dodged the attack and the Howler monkeys began to scream out at me. I yelled back at them and they all went silent again, which I don't think they were expecting. All at once they jumped up and scrambled running and hopping from tree branch to tree branch. I ran after them.

... The chase was on.

I've never been a fast runner but those monkeys I think liked being chased because every time they got a bit ahead of me the whole group slowed down. I watched them jump up and slide down, grab on vines and even push each other off the branches. Some of them lost balance and fell off the branch but in a flash their tail caught the branch and boom they were back up again.

Have you ever been chased by someone, maybe you were playing tag or did something awful to someone. Well I can remember a few times in my life me and a few of our friends being chased down. It always happened this way, we start off altogether but in one quick moment everyone runs one way and I run the other direction, alone. It's terrible because usually the group chasing us runs after the lone person. Somehow I always managed to get away.

Those particular howlers must have got tired of playing around, because all at once they shot off in a direction. And one lonely monkey decided he was going to go in the opposite direction. Just like me, so I followed him. I noticed two things about this particular monkey, one it wasn't playing around. It looked at me momentarily and when it did I could see fear in its eyes. The second thing I noticed was that it was slowing down and taking big gasps of breath. I slowed my pace and as I did his howls turned to cries. I wanted to chase monkeys, I didn't want to scare them. I began to feel really bad, was I making this monkey feel like it was alone?

"Hey" I yelled out.

The monkey stopped, turned around looking at me it was quivering in fear.

"I'm sorry. You don't have to be scared, I'm going back now."

I looked up at him and it stared right back at me, catching its breath with its little black eyes scanning me and the world around. I turned around to walk away. Something hit me in the head, hard. I grabbed my head and seen a stick hit the ground. I turned around and looked up at the monkey, I swear it let out a laugh and, in a flash, vanished into the jungle.

Later that day I was playing games with the kids out in a field when one of them screamed and shouted. He was off wandering near the edge of the field that was bordering the jungle. He was running quickly towards our direction, immediately 4 of the youth not older than 10 picked up a stick they had laying on the side of the field and ran towards that young boy. I ran alongside them and seen the boy being chased by a very small looking black snake. He was scared you could see it in his face.

"LABARAIS!" one of the kids cried out.

Now the Labaria's is one of the world's most deadly poisonous snakes, there are two types of labaria a large one and a small one. The larger ones can control the venom they inject within you and if bitten you're chances of living are slim to none. I know it doesn't sound like much but at least it gives you a fighting chance, its not much but you still have a chance. The smaller ones however, cannot control how much venom they inject so they poison you with every ounce they carry and as a result almost all bites are fatal. This young man was being chased by a small Labaria. Every step counted and you could see the sheer panic in his face.

The sticks that the kids had I was later told were snake sticks, roughly about 3 feet long so when a poisonous snake would strike to attack, you had some leeway to avoid the bite. I was scared and couldn't quite tell you why I was following alongside these boys. They rushed up and as the snake saw the four boys and immediately turned around to head back to the jungle. The boys followed in pursuit until they caught up to the snake. I remember I could feel its fear as the boys neared and they struck it. Over and over again until it stopped moving. I wanted to tell them not to kill it but I was a foreigner and this was their land and their law. Still I couldn't stop feeling its fear but I was glad they had killed it quickly. The little boy ran all the way home to tell his father. I remember standing there with the boys as we looked at this snake, they didn't say anything. I bent down and picked it up its body full of smooth scales rested in my hands. I was expecting it to be warm but it was cool to the touch.

Just then the young boys father appeared and he was livid.

"Why did you kill that snake?" He was yelling looking at me shaking his finger.

Before I could say anything the boys jumped in.

"He did no such thing. It was us, we killed it because it was chasing your son!"

"This snake is my brother and you know it. You could have just chased him back into the jungle, where he belongs."

"Yeah but."

"No, there is nothing for you to tell me. My brother, that snake has taken many lives even from my own family. But still I love him even if I don't always understand my brother. You, me and this jungle are all connected. Just because you can kill doesn't mean you should."

Tears formed in their eyes.

"I'm sorry" each said.

"It is my brother whom you should apologise to. And you! What are you doing?"

I looked at him and looked at the snake, his head was in my hands and his body in my other hand.

"I'm going to bury him and pray that he finds his way home."

Just as I said that even though his body was lifeless, his tail curled around my wrist and for a moment it was tight then it released itself. I was surprised and freaked out, I almost dropped the snake.

The man looked at me and his expression didn't change he just nodded.

"Go then and bury our brother."

I walked and entered the jungle, I was told not to go too far in because the further you went in the more dangerous it became. I bent down and found some soil, there was a long line of ants marching and each held some leafs on their heads carrying it back to the colony. It was the perfect place to bury him but I needed the ants to move. I thought of Sequoyah and what he might say to me. I thought to myself

"I guess I could ask these ants to move, there would be no harm in it. They might listen and they might not." For the record I felt a little crazy for even thinking about asking them. I bent down and I began to speak but I thought my voice is probably loud to these little ants, so I whispered.

"Excuse me" The ants stopped momentarily. "I don't mean to be a bother but I need to bury this snake and say a prayer. It'll only take a minute. I was wondering if you could please move until I'm done."

The ants stopped looked at each other one by one, then they began to walk. Slowly they walked around the area I was going to dig.

"Thanks."

I dug a hole and placed the snake into it.

"I'm sorry you died with fear in your heart. I'm sorry I didn't speak out. I'm sorry they didn't chase you back into the jungle. But thank you, thank you for your life. I ask that you are guided to find your way back home. Please forgive us for taking your life in this way. It's time to go home now. You've done your job."

I placed the earth onto the snake and push the dirt on top of its body and whispered to the ants.

"Thank you."

Slowly they began to take back their original trail as I walked back to the camp.

Night fell quickly, quicker than usual and I came upon my hammock. My friend was sitting there like she was waiting for me. In her hands she had two pieces of fruit, things I had never seen before. They didn't even have English names. It was in the shape of a star, they were red like strawberries but the skin was that of a peach. It was juicy and sweet, just thinking about it makes my mouth water.

"When are you leaving?" she asked.

I was having so much fun I forgot to keep track of time. I knew I would have to return sooner or later it was always at the back of my head.

"I was trying not to think about it. But now that you bring it up. In a couple days I will be leaving."

"Would you ever stay?"

I thought about staying, that thought crossed my mind a few times.

"I don't know."

"Do you like it here?"

The jungle has a magic to it a life you can't find anywhere else on this planet. It creeps up on you and when you think of all those beautiful moments at once you realise...

"I love it here. Everything that happens from sun up to sun down."

"The kids love you too. The boys are always telling stories of that crazy giant man."

"I love those kids."

"Well then why not stay?"

I looked at my fruit studying it before I took a bite. Never have I ever had anything so delicious.

"I don't know."

One of my faults is sometimes when the most obvious occurrences are happening I'm completely oblivious.

"Where would I stay?"

"Here. With me."

She had these beautiful caring eyes that commanded your utmost attention. A voice that was both gentle and strong.

Beauty emanated with every fabric of her being from head to toe. If she was here in North America she would be a definite model. The type of woman who could have any man just by throwing her gaze and here she was looking at me.

Everything she was saying was starting to make a lot of sense. The idea of living there and growing old all made sense, I didn't know if it was her eyes or the magic cast from the jungle maybe it was both. I was quickly being sold on the idea of life in the jungle.

"What about coming back home with me?"

"I hate the cities every single one I've ever been to. Listening to your stories of the cities up north there all the same boring and not real. Here in this place you can touch the ground, feel its warmth and its love. This is real. This is where I want to be."

There was no changing her mind.

"I'd have to think about it."

She looked at me without changing her expression and took one last bite of her fruit.

"Thank you for your visit."

She got up and left. I never seen her again after that, I didn't know if she was avoiding me or wanted me to seek her out. I would have and I wanted to but I needed some time to think. Part of me wanted to stay and another part wanted to go. I was making plans in my head to stay and how I would stay. Some nights just have a strange way to sway your mind.

THREE OF THE FOUR

The funny thing about most dreams is not being able to tell that you're dreaming -- even when the most peculiar unrealistic thing happens.

I was walking down a road I had never been before but everything felt familiar. I don't think I was lost I was just walking. I could see the blue pavement under my feet and heard the sounds of planes and aircraft flying over. Out in the distance I could see a massive city with mountains behind it. I didn't notice it at first but every step I had taken was bringing me further into the ground. Like the pavement became a type of mud without losing its texture but sucking me deeper. I was waist deep an unable to move. I blinked as I did I was now in the jungle wrapped in vines, still unable to move. These vines had wrapped my arms and legs and body even my head was stuck. I was feeling completely uncomfortable every time I tried to move the vines wrapped tighter and tighter. I wanted to scream out but when I opened my mouth no sounds came out. Everything was quiet. The world itself darkened and I couldn't see anything. Then I heard a hissing, a deep long hissing. Everything around me began to lighten up and when I was finally able to see I was deep within the jungle. A place I was told to avoid if I was on my own. The hissing came from somewhere in the thick brush. I was looking trying to find the sound, imagining a giant snake that would come crashing through the bush. On the ground a black line shot across and for a second it looked almost like a giant leg and foot but it was neither.

It was a tree that walked over roots and all. The tree extended a branch that stopped just an inch away from my face. Slowly the hissing sound returned and down the branch a black snake slithered. Not a very large one in fact it wasn't that big at all. But it was a Labaria, a small deadly Labaria. The vines held my body tightly, hopelessly I struggled. I could do nothing but watch as it silently edged its way towards me bobbing its head left to right.

The Labaria stopped inches away from my face licking the air and tasting the fear which had completely taken over my body. I didn't want to die and all it would take was just one venom filled bite. The snake hissed gently at first I was afraid and I couldn't look it in the eye. Then when I did I saw the bright yellow of his eyes and the sharp black slits that made its pupils. The snake cast a cold emotionless look my way. I didn't know what else do to at that moment.

"I don't know how I've gotten into this situation."
I took a deep breath and realised there was nothing I could do to change my circumstances.

"If you're going to bite me I can't stop that. My life is in your hands and if you chose to take it, then I won't be mad. I just wish I didn't have this fear."
The snake pulled its tongue back into its body almost as if to ingest my emotion. It blinked a few times then spoke.

"There is nothing to fear in death. The only thing you should fear is how you will die. I have a gift for you and some advice but first reach out and take it."
I looked and my left hand was no longer bound I reached out to the snake and in its tail it had an object wrapped in a leaf. The snake passed me the object.

"Put it in your pocket and don't forget about it. They will

ask you and you must show them."

"Who will ask?" I asked as I placed the object into my pocket.

It laughed.

"The journey you're on is strange. But the last one, the last one is going to hurt and you're going to learn so very much."

"What's going to hurt? What am I going to learn?"

"You cannot stay here anymore. You have to go home. Now wake and remember."

I opened my eyes and was lying in my hammock, it was the middle of the night. There was no around but the odd sounds of the nocturnal jungle. I pinched myself to see if I was truly awake or if I was indeed sleeping. It hurt. So I pinched again just for good measure. The second time really hurt. I got out of my hammock and ducked my head as I walked out of my wooden thatch house.

Looking up I saw the night sky, there are so many countless stars you can see when it's just you and the darkness. It reminds you of how utterly and terribly gigantic the universe really is and how small you actually are. I looked up in awe seeing stars and constellation, there was no moon that night. Then the far corner of the sky lit up like a bomb had went off. But it was no bomb, there was a thunder storm coming in except it was so far off all you could see was the light. The sky lit up again but from the opposite side of the horizon. I looked around and noticed that the storm clouds were surrounding the place I was standing. They formed a complete circle around the area. When I noticed that, lightening began to brighten up around all sides of me, some of it was pink and blue. Then faintly the rumbles of the thunder began, first as a low murmur than louder and louder like a lion. The clouds all began to draw near like a bird closing its wing. I closed my eyes as the rain began to pour down all over me. The rain drops were thick as it began to pour down by the buckets. I was getting soaked and feeling refreshed as I closed my eyes lightening lit up the sky once more followed by a loud roar.

Then all at once everything went quiet and the world around me yet again froze in time. The light was incredibly bright and the brightness was intensifying. I looked around and saw drops of rain suspended in the air I cupped my hands and began to collect the drops. I pushed them together creating a water ball in my hand in the same manner you would create a snowball. I looked at it as I shaped it into a perfectly round object as I could get it. Then I took a drink it was warm and a bit salty rainwater always tastes a bit different.

Then I heard a noise, it sounded like it was the thunder slowed completely down. It was hypnotic I could feel the slow vibration coursing through my veins. The world around me brightened up, I had to shut my eyes. It was like the light entered my body from head to toe as a feeling came over me. It was understanding what adventures were made of. It was a feeling of wonder, a feeling that would help lead my decisions from here on in, underneath and within everything is love.

...I had found the third star

Yet I still felt like a piece of me was missing.

THE BUILDING ROOM

I was in the dark black room looking down at the concrete slab examining the corpus. I could see the shapeless formless thing. I wanted to touch it again like I did so many years ago. It looked like it would be soft, warm and gooey. I reached out my hand and just before I touched it.

"HEY!"

I turned around saw the old man.

"I swear I turn my back for one second and you start trying to touching things and trying to break things."

"I wasn't trying to break it." I responded

The old man just looked at me shaking his head.

"Do you remember the last time you looked up at the stars? I mean really gazed up at the heavens?" He pointed up and as I looked up I could see the stars, I could see into the cosmos, I could see into nebulas and I could see moons of all shapes, sizes and colours. Moons made of fire, ice, gold and substances I never knew existed.

"To be reminded of how insignificant we really are in the whole grand scheme of things? And at the same time, to also be reminded how important we are in the whole grand scheme of things? When was it that you spent quality time with the night sky and the stars above?"

It was something I had just done but aside from that it was something I seldom ever did.

"You might be wondering why it's important to lift your head and raise your eyes to the stars. It's simple because they've always been there watching over you, a silent partner and a support when you needed one."

"My whole life they've watched over me?"

I began to think back when I was a kid waiting for the stars.

"Yes. Stars fall every now and again from the heavens just like angels. And they fall for a number of reasons. Sometimes they fall to earth and sometimes they fall beyond. And if they land on earth they become a great many things."

I thought about how the first was a star lying on top of a hill, how the second was a man and the third was a storm.

"They have an important job as stars with its duties, obligations and responsibilities, after all it is also the oldest job."

"Which is?"

"To create and sustain life. They're also loved and admired by all living beings in creation. But one day, one moment, one brief microsecond they choose to give that job up and they begin to fall."

"I wonder what that feels like?"

"What, what feels like?"

"To be a star while it falls"

"I couldn't tell you. We'll never know and we will never understand. Many women and men have perished this earth searching for their stars. So you have to be careful. Promise?"

"Promise."

"As for wrecking that." The room went completely black again and the old man pointed to the corpus to the shapeless formless thing.

"You would have wrecked it. It's in a very important and delicate stage of growth. So keep your claws to yourself."

"Got it."

"Now since you're here I'm guessing you've collected something and you're here to present it?"

"Yeah."

"Well don't let me slow you down."

I closed my eyes and thought back to the jungle and said.

"Underneath and within everything is love."

When I opened my eyes I was holding the star, I walked over to the corpus and placed the star down. The thing wasted no time absorbing it.

The old man clapped his hands.

"Marvelous. Now be off."

Again he walked me to the door and pushed me back out.

DREAMS, VISIONS AND UNUSUAL
LANDS

I came back to Canada and started working with kids, but instead of being in the jungle I wanted to work everywhere all across the country. I would look to the horizon and picture that last of the four stars falling. I wanted to find it, inside I was always restless because finding that next star began to consume me. There was nothing anyone could say or do to calm me down. I would stay in one area and work for a bit and then move onto the next. I worked in the mountains, the deep forests, cities both big and small. The kids and I climbed mountains, hiked through and around the bush, made fires and played games. I met a whole bunch of youth with beautiful hearts and strong spirits. After a while a time came and I started working within the cities first on one coast but I quickly got bored and moved to the other.

But I didn't just work with kids. When you spend time on the land you begin to develop a relationship with it. Everywhere I had went, I seen the same story play out over and over again, watching the destruction of the earth. I got to hear the stories of change from something beautiful and pristine that could give and sustain life into an industrialization that took all life. It got me interested and I attended gatherings and went to events and heard people speak of a thing called sustainability which I felt meant a brighter future for all of us. Eventually people would ask me about the place I grew up and the changes I had seen. They must have liked my story because more and more people got to fly me out to different places. I almost always said yes, after all each flight sent me out into the horizon and with each trip a chance to possibly find that next star.

It wasn't too long before I realised that flying everywhere is pretty bad for the environment. So, I said yes less and less but every time I did I got a little more restless and little more anxious. I packed my bag and left again, eager to see what the world was going to bring me.

I traveled again and ended up far out east to the land of the Haudenosaunee and worked with more kids as we lived in ceremony. I helped them as they spread prayer, songs, laughter, love and hope. It was a pilgrimage. Our indigenous brothers and sisters in those nations carried a strength and pride I had never experienced before. In this pilgrimage we would run from one Haudenosaunee nation to another in unity praying for a better tomorrow.

It was weird to be out there because I certainly wasn't Haudenosaunee and I certainly wasn't related to anyone by blood. Each night we set up tents and made a fire, I heard stories of creation, destruction and life in between. I even told a few stories and played a lot of games with the kids. One day one of the kids ran up and called me 'Uncle' after that, everyone was calling me uncle.

We did a lot of running, we ran in the morning before sunrise, we ran under the hot afternoon sun and we ran sometimes well into the night. We each took turns and ran our hearts out when we got tired someone else took our place. It was done in a relay style, every day we started and ended with a prayer. Each night we were all tired and exhausted and I had to chase some kids to bed. At nights I would sit by the fire place after everyone had fallen asleep and I would look to the stars. The restlessness grew inside.

One morning we had an elder come by, he prayed over us. Then afterwards when everything was done he walked over to me and said.

"You're not done looking yet are you?"

"...No"

"Have faith, keep looking and you'll find it."

And with that he walked away. The day passed quickly and I stretched out by the fire and looked to the nights' sky.

...I fell into a deep sleep...

I was outside again that two storey red house which was perched on top of a hill, with the two bird brothers but they were nowhere to be seen. Again, it was neither day nor night, the world was just after sunset and right before sunrise. I saw the toys I played with as a kid, sitting in the yard. They were untouched even though it had been years it looked like I had just placed them down.

I thought of that beautiful Tipi and the strange shadows that were cast on the see through walls. I turned around and there it stood just as amazing and mysterious and just down the path. I left the yard of that house closing the gate and journeyed down the path, the closer I got the more the Tipi seemed to grow. It was now a giant structure with an entrance that was almost hidden. I could faintly see the outline of the door as I walked towards it. I saw an enormous buffalo hide door with three giant beasts that perched around the doorway. A Grizzly Bear which stood just to the side of the door, A Cougar that laid in front and a Snake which laid coiled around the tipi above the door. At first glance they looked like perfect statues. When I walked up to the door made of Buffalo hide, those statues moved.

"What are you doing here boy?" Questioned the Grizzly in a deep hoarse voice, it was the kind of voice that intimidated to your very core the kind of voice you'd expect a great Grizzly to have.

"... I dunno. I'm dreaming, I think." I responded

"Why have you come here? Why are you leaving the mind? Why are you here at the entrance to the heart of visions and dreams?" The Grizzly Asked

"I seldom choose where I want to go. I let spirit guide me from place to place." I explained

And the Grizzly laughed her laugh which was even deeper and scarier than when she spoke.

"Show me proof or I shall clean my teeth with your bones." The Grizzly opened its mouth and licked her lips.

I was terrified so very terrified, I didn't know how to show her proof and I certainly didn't want to be eaten. So I closed my eyes and thought back to the day near the jungle thinking that I would explain that day I found the third star. I opened my eyes as I was about to explain the story but I became incredibly nervous when I watched her lean in with her big grizzly mouth. She opened her mouth wide half of my body was able to fit into it. Nervously I began to rummage through my pockets looking for something, anything. In my pants pocket I felt something, it felt like a leaf. I reached in and pulled it out.

"What is this?"

I unwrapped the leaf. It looked almost like the shape of corn and it gave off a golden shine. It was hard like a shell and it was broken up into thirteen connected parts. The size also changed because it was now the same length as both of my hands. I shook it and the ground shook. It made the sound of a rattle. I looked again and realised within my hands I was holding a giant rattlesnake tail.

I looked up and seen the Grizzlies eyes widened, she closed her mouth and sat back on the door.

"Hmmm. He will see you." The Grizzly growled

The Tipi door unravelled itself open, I was expecting to see the inside, but all I could see was blackness.

The cougar purred loudly and spoke in a soft gentle yet powerful voice

"Do you know where you are?" The cougar asked

"I'm dreaming." I answered

"Yes, but do you know what is in there?" Asked the Cougar staring straight into my eyes.

"No."

"There are things in there. Ghost things and wicked things but also beautiful things and lovely things. Many will try and trick you, some will lie to you and some will try and harm you. Trust what brought you here but if you doubt it and then believe in that doubt, you will be lost and then you will die. Here anything and everything is possible, because anything and everything is real"

"...Is there anything else?" I asked

The Snake uncoiled itself and crawled down from the top of the entrance.

"Ssssstay on the path, it issss a red path. Don't wander off it no matter what you ssssee or hear, you will become losssst in dreams. Dreams guide and free you. Others become lost in Dreamsssss only to have them eat away and ssswallow you completely. Do not look at your reflection itsss not what it sssseemsss and no matter what you hear or sssssee ssssstay on the path...." It instructed licking the air.

I stood on the steps looking at the three beasts.

"Thank you"

THE LONGEST JOURNEY

I remembered its words as I passed through the door way and walked. I walked into the darkness and quickly realised the path turned into a road and it changed into numerous colours before finally settling on the colour red. The red road was wide in the beginning and easy to walk at first. Along the edges of the path I felt a wall made of rock, the inside of the tipi had now become a cave. The walls widened the further I walked, the edges expanded into the darkness until I could no longer see them. It was just me surrounded by darkness walking on this path.

In the blackness of the cave I heard a small whimpering it came from something small and on the ground. I bent down and felt around on the ground until I felt something small and furry, I could also feel a tail.

"Ew! A mouse?" I stammered freaking out

"IS that how you talk to an Elder?" The mouse responded

"An Elder" I said in surprise still holding the mouse in front of my face.

"Yes an Elder. I am a grandmother don't cha know." She spoke very calm. Each time she did she felt less like a mouse and more like a Grandmother. The kind of warm feeling only a family member can bring.

"I didn't know. I'm sorry." I looked around seeing nothing but the darkness. "What are you doing here?"

"What's wrong with right here?"

"It's really dark, it's almost pitch black."

"Is it? Well it's not like it even matters anyways. The Darkness has never slowed me down. But now it's a bit different isn't it."

"What's a bit different?"

"I don't have my eyes anymore."

"Oh my goodness! What happened? How did you lose them?"

"HA! I didn't lose them. I gave them away."

I found it hard to believe you could give away something like your eyes.

"How did you manage that? Our eye balls are stuck in their sockets."

"My dear Grandson. You can give anything of yours away. You can also lose anything of yours as well, for great reasons and for foolish reasons."

"Why did you give your eyes away?"

"I took pity on a wolf that was blind and starving. He was careless with the things he was looking at and because of that he lost his eyes."

"Aren't you worried that he'll be careless with your eyes?"

"I can't very well be worried about things that are completely out of my hands."

"Hmm. Where are you going? Maybe I can help you."

"I'm going where ever Creator guides me."

"Yeah, me too. I think"

"Well I'd love to join you. But I think I'll wait here just a little longer if it's all the same to you."

"Are you sure?"

"Yeah. I'm still waiting on something."

"Ok. Be safe Grandmother."

"Take care Grandson."

That warm feeling a grandparent brings quickly left as I walked away from the Grandmother. What had filled that void was a lonely lingering feeling that seemed to grow with every step I took.

The path itself was never straight for too long it took many twists and turns. Sometimes the path would dip down only for a moment and then quickly rise, ascending was twice as hard. It's an interesting thing to be walking in the darkness every time I felt like quitting, the path would level out and walking became easier. Thoughts would creep up, positive and negative but I kept walking thinking to myself I have to get to the heart of dreams and visions. I walked on for what seemed forever, many hours and when I got tired I laid down it was warm enough to sleep but it wasn't comfortable. Days passed by.

Sometimes other paths would present themselves just a little off the red road. Some pathways were paved of gold and jewels, but those quickly turned into sand as I passed by. Others led to what looked outside into the most beautiful of gardens. I could hear animals, monkeys and even saw spiders singing ring around the rosy. This grey and white cat walked up to me pointed and laughed. The road quickly began to thin out becoming as tiny as a thread that slanted down to either side. It was a hard balancing act as it was easy to slip off but I knew I was getting closer.

Then the road widened and dipped again, the climb up was almost unbearably steep. I would lose my footing and fall momentarily losing whatever ground I had just gained. The feeling of quitting overwhelmed my mind and I fell to my knees questioning to myself why I was on this road and where it would ultimately take me. I was expecting something to make the journey easier, but the air cooled to an uncomfortable degree as I felt a cold chill travel to the bone. Snow began to fall. I was freezing, tired and lost, surrounded by the darkness.

I turned around to see how far I was and when I looked back to the entrance of the Tipi Cape, it was literally only a few steps behind. For all that traveling I didn't really get that far. I was completely disheartened and had made up my mind to quit. I got up and just before I took my first step back, I heard whimpering. It didn't sound like a human it sounded like it came from a dog. I turned around facing towards the heart of dreams and visions, upwards on the path just to the side was a Coyote. He or she was hurt and bleeding from its leg I couldn't help but feel pity as I began walking towards it.

When I came upon the Coyote I leaned into to give it a pet not sure what I could do to comfort it, the best thing I figured was to give it love. As I was petting it, I began to sing a hand drum song. I looked at the wound on its leg blood was trickling out. I ripped a piece of my shirt off and wrapped it around its leg.

"Aww, what happened to you lil buddy?" I asked

The coyote sat up looking into my eyes

"A group of foxes came and took away my five children, I tried to protect them but they overwhelmed me. Now I lie here waiting for death to take me. My children are gone and I have nothing." Spoke the coyote in between whimpers.

I thought that was kind of weird since foxes are very small and this coyote was a lot bigger than foxes I had seen.

"When did this happen?"

"Moments ago, if you listen you can hear them laughing."

I sat with the coyote and listened we heard the low hum of laughter coming from out in the distance.

"Well... let's go get them."

"I can reward you if you come with me, my den is full of what your people consider treasures"

"Let's not worry about that, lets just get them back."

"Ok, follow me."

The Coyote looked at me like it was smiling, it had a mischievous look like she was hiding something or maybe she was just happy to have someone rescue her children. She ran off the path and as she did a new path presented itself appearing out of nowhere. The ground was soft and made of moss, 'easy walking' I thought to myself. In the darkness I could see a spec of light as we were coming to an exit the world got warmer. As we got to the exit I could see the sun shining, outside was the most beautiful old growth forest I have ever seen. The Coyote turned around.

"Your Mother and your Fathers' original indigenous languages are exactly like this old growth forest. Older than time itself, it is the way the spirits talk, for the spirits speak the original tongue. Do you know what gave birth to your language?"

"No."

"The spirit world and the land gave birth to your ancestor's language. Secrets and gifts about the natural world around you can be found within your Blackfoot or Dene dialect. It is important for us not to lose that connection. However all places around the world speak a different tongue. I don't know why there's so many languages but I do know that each language has different secrets and gifts to offer. That world is an interesting being, revealing nothing to one but everything to all. To achieve peace all that you people have to do is share with one another."

Her voice was rhythmic, comforting and hypnotic. I couldn't help but listen.

"Did you know when your spirit came into this world, the world was waiting for you to greet it in the tongue of the spirits. The earth is sad when you cannot converse with it in your original language."

The more she spoke to me, the further we got away from the path that led to the heart of the dreaming.

"What about English?" I asked

The coyote laughed

"Almost everything about the English language is dead, it over simplifies everything as this world around you is very, very complex. Yet it's not complex at the same time, not when you learn to speak with it."

"But, what are languages?"

"Languages are just different dialects of love. The place we all come from, the sky world is made from that very word, Love. When you're there you're wrapped within love. It's a place that never lose that feeling, it never loses its novelty or meaning, this truth exists not just in the sky world or in the dream world, but in the waking world as well. However, on your earth people always forget about that or feel like they are not worthy of love. You human beings are strange and pitiful creatures. Must be why the spirits favour you."

I could hear laughter of the foxes grow as we came upon a little mound which was surrounded by bushes. The Coyote stopped and dropped to its belly, I did they very same thing. I could hear myself breathing loudly as my heart was racing. The Coyote whispered

"Where about to come upon the foxes, you rush them and I'll gather my young."

I couldn't quite make out the foxes that were just on the other side of the mound, the brush was thick all around us. I looked over at the Coyote and watched it take deep breaths in and release slowly. I did the same and my heart began to slow down.

"How many of them are there?"

"About 7 or 8. Are you ready?"

"Ok, give me a second"

I thought about the Grizzly bear, the Cougar and the giant Snake and how terrifying they were. I wanted to become as fearsome as those animals or at least think I was as ferocious. I could hear the foxes bragging about killing the mother Coyote as they were about to eat her young. I looked over at the Mother and she gave me a wink, I jumped up letting out the most terrifying scream I could muster. I was expecting to see regular small sized foxes that I could easily chase away. My heart froze at the sight, I was mistaken they were not foxes at all but were giant Black and Grey wolves. Seven or eight very large wolves as big as me, maybe even bigger. They were all very hungry and all very mad at the same time.

I managed to startle them all at first, some even jumped out of fear but anger over took their emotions when they saw who startled them as they rushed me. I looked at those young babies and a sense of strength grew inside, nothing was going to stop me from protecting them. They charged me and I charged right back, I could see some licking their lips anticipating a quick kill. I knew that this charge would most certainly end me and that the wolves would run me down and then feast like kings. But those young ones and their cries kept me moving forward. The biggest wolf was also the one closest to me, I looked him straight in the eyes as he pounced and not once did I look away. If I was going to meet death I was going to look it right in the eyes. The moment before he made contact he vanished into a puff of smoke. The rest scattered and ran away into different directions. The Coyote mother came and gathered all her young, each untouched and resting on her back.

"Follow me! Quick to the Den!" She instructed.

We ran till we came to a great tree with a top so high it disappeared into the clouds, at the base within that tree was her den. Inside the den there were no great treasures to see, just the mud of the earth and the roots of the tree. My Mothers words echoed on inside me, 'Sometimes people lie or fib to make things better than they seem.'

One by one she passed her pups and I placed them near a root and tucked them away carefully. They felt odd, heavier than I could have figured a coyote pup should weigh and also very cold. Even though I could see them and hear them sleeping they appeared lifeless especially at how cold they were. Once her young were all settled in and sleeping, I looked at the Coyote.

"You lied about the foxes, these pups and treasures inside your house."

The Coyote looked at me.

"Would you have followed me if I told you the truth?"

"Yeah, you needed help. I mean, I thought you needed help. Sometimes it is best to give without thinking."

"I did, I needed help saving my pups."

"And since when were Rocks considered pups?" I asked as I looked back at the roots where I placed each pup, I could see Rocks of different colours shapes and sizes in their place. The image of young pups were all just an illusion.

The Coyote looked at me and was smiling if such a thing was

possible.

"And although this is a very beautiful home and it is a true treasure, it's not the treasure that most human beings seek."

The Coyote began to laugh

"Hmm, well I present you with three different options. You can stay here in this den with me for as long as you want or I can show you a short cut around the red road and take you directly to the heart of dreams and visions or I can lead you back the way you came."

"I could stay here with you for as long as I wanted, my home is in my heart. But that's not why I am here. I am here to see what awaits me at the heart of dreams and visions. A shortcut would be nice but something tells me it's more of your lies and trickery... I'll just go back the way I came."

"So, you will continue on with your journey?"

"Yes. I have to see where that red road takes me and I fear I ventured off the path long enough."

The Coyote laughed again

"You are right to stay away from the affairs of Coyotes and our business. There is no short cut on this red road, no matter what anyone tells you... But I cannot take you back the way you came. You have to find your own way back and if you don't you will be lost out here forever."

My heart froze up.

"Why? Why have you led me here just to abandon me?"

"It's my job as a coyote it's my nature to be a Trickster."

I took a deep breath and looked at it without anger or frustration and smiled.

"Thank you."

"Thank you? You're not mad at me?" it asked.

"I suppose I can't be if you're just doing the job your put on this world to do. I can be no madder at you than I could be for the sun rising and setting every day."

I grabbed its face and stuck my forehead to its furry forehead and took a deep breath, took a deep breath and then let go.

"I forgive you. But tell me, before you leave me why is

this path so hard?"

"It's hard because it is supposed to be. Because it is the longest trip on the shortest journey."
She looked at me and sighed.

"The only hint I can give you is to close your eyes."
I didn't quite know what she met and right before my eyes she began to fade away.

"When it gets hard, be thankful. This path is open to everyone but seldom do people choose to walk it...This is as far as I go, and remember if you get back, <u>Stay on the Path!</u>"
I left the den and looked out into the vast never ending wilderness, the trees must have moved around because the landscape did not look the same. A sombre wind hit me, the kind of cool wind that normally comes with fall. I looked up at the sky and the clouds, then to my feet where the earth was, I looked over both my shoulders and then forward squinting my eyes to see as far as I could, nothing but bush. I took a deep breath as despair began to take over, I sat down and lowered my head placing my hand on my heart and remembered.

"Well, you're good and lost." I heard a familiar voice say.
I looked up and seen an older man walking, he had long flowing white hair. It took me a couple of seconds to recognize him and when I did I was in utter disbelief.

"Sequoyah?"
He let out a laugh.

"Haha, yep."

"Is it really you? What are you doing here?"

"It's really me. I'm no dream thing like everything else that's around us. What am I doing here? I'm here to help!"

"How did you know I needed help?"

"I didn't know it was you that needed help. I listened and spirit guided me here."

"Well I think we both need help now. The statues told me I wasn't supposed to venture off the path and if I did I would be lost forever."

"Why did you leave the path?"

"I listened to this coyote and she tricked me to follow her out here."

"Tricksters often lead people astray. What did she say to lead you off the path and out here?"

"We were supposed to rescue her children. I forgot about the rules to not leave the path, the things she told me on our way here was incredible."

He smiled at me.

"Tricksters often use their words and truth to lead us astray."

"So you've been here before?"

"Plenty of times. I love it out here."

I looked at him

"How do I get myself out of this situation?"

He looked at me and responded.

"Trust in spirit. Spirit will never misguide you or misdirect you. I got myself lost out here once and then I had to get myself un lost. You are going to have to do the same thing."

He got up dusted himself off he looked around and then out into the distance.

"Are you going to help me get un lost?"

"Nope. You're going to have to find your way out of here."

"What if I can't find my way out of here?"

"I did and what one of us can do we all can."

He gave me a wink and in a flash he was gone again, he made it look like child's play. I sat there looking around I had a little bit of hope.

I said out loud what the Coyote spoke to me.

"The only hint is to close your eyes."

I thought about that for a while then I closed my eyes. I began to visualise the path and the cave, beneath myself I could feel the cave begin to materialise it was surreal.

"How do I get out of here?" I said to myself

"It's simple you just have to remember" An old voice whispered.

I opened my eyes and looked around, I was still outside in the bushes I could hear a rustle in the trees and looked up I seen nothing but the ruffling of wings. I closed my eyes again and began to visualize the path, the cave and the darkness. I stood up.

"Trust in spirit."

I took a step and when I opened my eyes I was back on the Red Road and again surrounded by the darkness.

THE SHORTEST DISTANCE

It was still snowing on the path and still very cold, it was just bearably warm and I don't know if that made things worse. During the climb up the path only got steadily steeper. In the distance I could hear faint rumbles of roars or thunder I couldn't quite make out the sounds but I kept climbing and climbing. Again the feelings of quitting were persistent, but the Coyotes words came back every time I wanted to quit, "It's hard because it is supposed to be." I said my prayer of thanks and remembered to trust in spirit. I kept venturing forth.

After a while the path levelled out again and then came into a hall full of mirrors with lanterns hanging . Above the room storm clouds gathered, they blotted out the lights and made everything in the room almost pitch black. Lightening was striking all around and the thunder shook the very room. I was scared but I knew I had to go forward, I knew my direction I looked down at the path and focused real hard on the road. There were times where I almost could not see it.

Everything went completely silent even the sounds of my foot steps as they made contact with the ground. The silence was piercing and terrifying at the same time. I could do without sight, against the cold and fighting thoughts of self-doubt. But the silence began to vanquish my spirit. The unnerving feeling inside grew with every step. The only thing I could hear was the sound of my breath inhaling and exhaling, I took small refuge in that. It was the faintest bit of hope and the only thing that kept me teetering on the edge of madness.

And then that was taken as the darkness had engulfed me.

There is nothing more frightening than having your senses stolen from you. I was lost in every meaning and definition of the word. I couldn't see and now I couldn't hear. You'd be surprised how fast doubt can take over your thoughts when your world is suddenly flipped upside down. I was moving forward yet taking very small steps.

"Where was I? What was I doing?" It was a thought that once popped up I couldn't push back down.

For a moment I couldn't answer that question and stopped walking. I didn't know if I was asleep, in a coma or dying.

"Was this what it was like to go crazy?" I wondered to myself

I was surrounded in the silence and the darkness. There was nothing I could change and in the moment I accepted it. I was in the darkness and I was the darkness.

"Look at me" a voice whispered from the walls

'Forget about the path' another voice shouted.

'Come Play' 'You're good for nothing' 'Let's go party' 'You'll never make it' 'You don't got what it takes'

Sometimes those voices sounded like people I knew, friends, family and sometimes those voices I heard sounded like me.

A part of me wanted to quit. The voices from the walls scared me, walls shouldn't have voices and they shouldn't talk. One thing was for sure, I didn't want to stay in this area.

I took a step forward and the world slowly began to lighten around me. Like maybe I was glowing. The path returned and to the left and right of me I could see the wall were gigantic mirrors. As soon as I realised they were mirrors I looked back to the red road and walked.

When I think about that dream, I think maybe all those voices from the mirrors were mine. Everything that was spoken resonated within me, they reflected all my doubts and all my fears. Dreams are funny things.

I came upon two great doors, they seemed bigger than the Tipi itself. They were huge and beautiful and changed colour and texture. The road seemed to get a little wider the closer I got. When I got close enough a smaller door within those doors opened up. Behind me a Crow or Raven cawed out, I entered the room.

In the far back of this grand room, I saw a giant man tall as a tree dressed all in Black and White Buckskin with enormous windows behind him. Those windows looked out into space, into the cosmos and into our planet. He got off his chair walking towards me, with every loud step he looked like he was growing smaller. For every step I took towards him, he took two towards me. By the time we reached one another, he was just a little taller than I and he had these beautiful brown eyes that spoke to me of age and of wisdom.

"Do you know who I am?" He asked

"… Napi?" Somehow looking at him I just knew

He let out a smile

"And what do you know of me?"

"You're either a young man or an elder. But you helped to shape the world through stories, legends, dreams and visions. You were there when life first started."

"That is correct"

"Why am I here?" I asked

"You trust in your dreams"

"And my dreams have brought me here?" I inquired

"Your dreams will take you anywhere and everywhere. Sometimes even the lowest of low places. But within it, is a story."

"Every one of your stories has a morale" I added

"As does yours?"

"I wandered off the red road. I saw a lot of other trails."

He reached out and touched my head. In my mind I saw the red road and all the twists and turns it has, although they all branched out from one another, they all formed one big road in the end.

"All pathways lead to me, sooner or later."

"Are you really Napi, is this really happening?" I questioned

"I am Napi, Your people have heard all my stories but I'm also interested in hearing yours."

"Are you here to tell me my future?" I asked

"No, I'm not as a seer. If I wanted to I could look and tell you all about your birth, life and death. but I won't. My world is of dreams and visions. I am here to help you listen to yours."

"That's good, cause I don't really want to know all that. I just have a few questions."

"When you were a boy, you saw four stars fall to the ground."

"Yeah, I have a hard time remembering that when I am awake but when I'm sleeping I remember like it just happened."

"What would you like to know about the next one?"

"I don't want to know how to find it. I like how they've just been popping up randomly in my life. But I've got a warning saying this next one will hurt. What does that mean? What will hurt?" I asked with uncertainty

"What do you know of love?"

"Nothing much, I was in love once before." I explained

"Well let me tell you this. Some Love lasts for just a brief moment, Some Love lasts a lifetime, some through several lifetimes as it stretches out into eternity. Remember you are a human being, a simple human and everything sooner or later ends. It is what makes everything in your world special. Everything physical perishes, you can't keep a favourite anything around forever. And the things you can't see, those feelings you have inside they have so much more meaning, such as love. The only thing you can do is cherish those moments when they happen."

I sat down and didn't say a thing. As I sat, a fire formed in front of me, and a plot of earth and dirt encased around the fire. The rest of the floor turned into yellow grass, it was no longer a cave floor. When I looked around, I saw Canvas walls made from buffalo hide, with wooden poles all around. When I looked up I saw the sky and realised I was sitting inside a Tipi.

Napi was sitting across the fire, dressed in black with a brown bag made of hide beside him.

"Love is like this fire, sometimes the person you fall in love with, their fire is wild and out of control. They can burn you and they can hurt you, in fact those fires hurt the world around them. Some fires can warm you, nurture you and light your way. If you take care of this fire, it'll take care of you."

"So I just feed it but what do you feed love?" I asked

"Yourself. However, you must watch how you feed it. And when you're in love you're always feeding it. Every stick you place into this fire is attached with an emotion, if you're mad or angry that's what you'll place into this fire. That can make this fire grow out of control, can make it dangerous, to yourself, the world around you and especially the one you love."

I sat there looking at him.

"Your star is a cub but it isn't what you think it is and only when this is all over, it will all make sense. The pain is the lesson."

"… A cub?" I said surprised

"Yes, you are an easy person to love. He will test you, he will learn from you and most importantly he will love you. All you have to do is be a man."

Napi reached into the bag and pulled out some dried meat.

"This is dream food, some original buffalo meat from a time when your ancestors lived by it. There's not too much of this stuff around. When you eat this you'll remember the dream and what I am about to say."

"For every step you take towards your dreams and towards creator. They'll take two steps towards you."

"Do you know what the longest journey is with the shortest distance?"

I looked back towards the entrance of the tipi and then at the fire and answered him.

Napi looked at me and smiled satisfied with the answer. He broke a piece of the dried meat and handed it to me. It was the most delicious thing I ever ate. A great many more things happened within that dream and most I forgot upon waking and some I've forgotten as time passed.

THE LAST STAR

I can't remember where I was living back then but it doesn't really matter because I packed my bags and headed out the door. I was off again and things had changed inside, my outlook in life was different. For all the other stars I was excited and eager but for this one I held a lot of caution and fear in my heart. The words had repeated themselves cryptically that this last star would hurt the most. It's weird to be fearful of the future and yet still head towards it.

Streets and cities have a certain charm and some would say their own personality. But when you've been on the road for as long as I have they all became one of the same. Some places are sunny others are cloudy some are cold and others humid. I loved seeing the world but it seemed like things were losing their glow, losing their novelty. Still I would look out into the horizon and wonder where that last star was. I would still get a little excited to enter into a new city or a new land.

I was expecting things in my life to go great but things began to spiral downwards. I was in between jobs but that's just a fancy expression for being unemployed. Work can do a lot for man, it tends to give a sense of purpose and yet there I was wandering around looking for something that might never appear. Some people can search their whole lifetime for a purpose and some carry on without a care. Some people can just be content with nothing or next to nothing. I had found three of the four stars and my desire to travel and find the last star was opposite from my desire to stay and create. I was constantly swinging like a pendulum in between my purpose and my desire. If that pendulum stopped it was only for a moment before it kicked out again.

In the middle of all of this that I had met your mother.

Your mother and I lived about 1500km away from each other we had met just one time and for me that's all it took. One day out of the blue we decided to meet each other somewhere in the middle. It was a city she had never been to and a city I didn't care too much to visit.

But why would I travel about 750km away to meet up with your mother? The answer is simple, a beautiful woman can often lead a man to do some very strange and often stupid things, without her even having to ask.

There I was, bags in hand as I arrived into the city mid-day and found my way down to a park. It would be a couple hours before you and your mother arrived so I waited and watched the sunset from a bench that overlooked the horizon. The sky went from light blue to dark and then one by one the stars began to present themselves. I had my travel bag on my back and a hot tea in my hand sitting, sipping and thinking. What if you didn't like me? What if we didn't get along? What if I let you down? Was I someone you would look up to?

Your mother had driven all day from where she lived to meet me in the middle of a city. It was going to be the first chance that I got to meet you. I had a nervous feeling that was running throughout my whole body, starting in the pit of my stomach and spreading out to the edges of my fingers and toes. I looked at my watch and was minutes away from seeing you and her.

I got off the bench and walked down the street to where your mother and I agreed to meet. Leaves were beginning to fall and collecting on the street. The autumn winds were but not quite blowing that cold bitter wind it was just on the cusp of that. The wind was warm and comforting almost inviting.

I turned a corner and saw a vehicle that was parked and waiting with a quiet low rumble. She flashed the lights as I walked towards her. I was just a few feet away when the front door opened up and your mom popped out. She had greeted me with a smile and I swear she has this thing that happens whenever she smiles. Your heart skips a beat. It might not make a lot of sense but allow me to explain.

There is not enough words in the English language to express how beautiful your mother is, she is beyond beautiful. Every time you look at her it's like you're looking at her for the first time and each time its captivating. She has a beauty that you could never get used to. Some women are just like that and to some people it freaks them out. An extremely beautiful woman can sometimes unknowingly bring out the insecurities of a man. You're mother has that ability. She also has these beautiful eyes that perfectly reflect innocence and passion. A smile that can melt hearts and give birth to butterflies in your stomach. Her face, well her face is like most wild and beautiful music you've ever heard.

It was her looks that brought me in but it was her wonderful heart and personality that hooked me. We could laugh and talk about anything, theorize about the future and joke about the past. In the end all it took was one kiss from her and I was hopelessly devoted. It's easy to fall in love with your mother, many a man have and many a man will. I still remember the first words she spoke to me.

"You're late."

"No I'm not."

"No need to lie about it."

"I'm not lying."

"It's ok I understand you got a little busy with other stuff like calling your current girlfriend and dumping her."

"I don't have a current girlfriend"

"Well not anymore you don't. She must have taken it pretty hard but I thank you for doing that I suppose. Kind of cold hearted but it also shows you got a bit of integrity and that my friend goes a long way."

"Integrity?"

"Yes."

"But, I didn't dump anybody."

"Look I get it that's why you're late. You're sorry, I'm sorry. So let's just start over."

And that was it, that's all it took. Seriously. I was hers, hook line and sinker hanging off her every word.

"You want to come meet my son?" she asked.

"Yeah sure, what's his name?"

She told me and it was a name I would never forget.

I remember the first time I met you. I don't think you knew quite what to make of me. I looked into the back of the vehicle you were in and saw this tiny little guy still in diapers strapped to a car seat. You had this cautious curious look on your face not quite sure of who I was or what I wanted. I stuck my hand out to shake yours and said

"Hello lil fella" I said my name as I introduced myself. "It's nice to meet'cha."

Your expression dropped the moment you reached your little hand out. Then you smiled and as you did the world lit up and everything around you brightened. Time froze yet again and nothing was moving but your little hand as it made its way to mine. I looked around at the world just momentarily, planes were suspended in the sky, people and traffic frozen. Do you know what a light looks like the moment when it turns on? I know because when I looked up I saw a traffic light in the midst of change. Light looks like an explosion it comes out like a fireball racing in all directions. But the light you were emitting kept calling out to me so I turned back to look at you and was completely blinded. I heard you laugh as that blinding light eclipsed everything.

You were the fourth star.

I had found the fourth star

or rather the fourth star had found me.

THE LIFE OF THE FOURTH

Love can make a sane person crazy and crazy person sane. Your mother and I decided pretty quickly that we were going to spend the rest of our lives together. Being young, dumb and in love we moved in together without really thinking it through. Love can also make people pretty stupid.

I want to say you and I hit it off right from the start but I had a feeling you were testing me out and didn't like me coming onto your territory.

I remember we were watching a TV show about talking trains, you were on the floor and me and your mother were on the couch. You stopped watching for a moment as an idea hit your head and then turned to look at me. There was a blank expression on your face and not one hint of malice. You got up and I thought you were heading to your room as you walked by me. The moment you had left my line of sight, I felt an intense pinch on my hand. I quickly looked down and there you were bent over trying to hide behind the couch and looking up at me. The moment our eyes met you were off running to your room.

Throughout the days sometimes you'd hurt or scare yourself and begin crying. I'd run over to pick you up and see if you were ok. You'd let me pick you up for just a second then you'd squirm yourself out of my arms and run for your mom. I felt a small bit of peace in those brief seconds you let me comfort you.

When your mom would cook for you wouldn't have any problems with anything. We'd sit you in your high chair and you would quiet down while eating every last drop. When I'd cook dinner you'd stand there and watch me make a mess of things. Dinnertime would come and then I'd have to chase you around to put you in your seat, you'd kick and struggle for a few seconds. Sometimes you would eat whatever I placed in front of you other times you wouldn't eat a thing. This one time you sat there looking at me not saying a thing just staring at me as I was eating. I looked over and when our eyes met, you picked up all your food and threw it onto the ground. I was beginning to think you had it in for me.

I have to admit though I loved every second of it. Everything you did was an equal mixture of cute and amazing. At the back of my mind I wondered if or when you ever going to open up to me.

One day I came into the room and watched as you played with trains. There was a train in each hand you were crashing them into each other.

"What'cha doing lil buddy?" I asked.

You looked at one train in your hand and then you looked at me and said my name as you handed it over.

I grabbed it and started making train sounds. We played crashing our trains into each other over and over again then chasing each other around the house and then finally putting them away. Being a dad was pretty sweet.

Every night before putting you to bed, I would read you a story. I had a collection of comic books and I always got you to pick out a story for me to read. I did voices and we looked at the pictures sometimes you would point at the things in the pictures and I would tell you what it was. Every night when I was done reading to you I would say

"Good night my boy."

And each night you would respond.

"Nighty Night."

Each time you did it made me feel like I was completing the most important job in the world. Like a bomb technician who cuts the right wire in one of those terrible action movies. It gave me the greatest sense of purpose.

Sometimes you would have the nightmares and they sounded terrible. I'd wake up hearing you scream and cry. Whenever I heard you I always jumped up and ran as quickly as I could. For a moment you'd let me hold you and then with your eyes shut tight you would begin to call out for your mother. I'd always bring you over to her and then suddenly and quietly you'd fall fast asleep. Then I'd return you to your bed. Some nights I would just peek in to check on you and see you sleeping peacefully.

I loved these little moments of waking up in the middle of the night. I held so much comfort being with your mother and you in the next room, it filled my heart and I felt like a complete being.

Mornings I would wake you up and get you ready for school, brush your hair and teeth, make you breakfast and send you off. I missed those days of waking you up and having you greet the new day. Sometimes you had the look of complete peace other times I could see a smile and I always wondered what kinds of dreams you were having.

Being around you made the whole world a better place to be in. I never knew life could have this kind of joy. Everything was just right.

INTERCHANGE

It was the middle of the night, I remember being asleep and it was like someone shook me wide awake. I swear I heard someone whisper to me "... and you're going to learn so very much". I had this feeling in the pit of my stomach that something had changed. I was getting used to the idea of staying around and being a husband and a father. I walked out of the bedroom and checked on you. You were sound asleep. I walked to the front door and opened it looking out into the sky, the stars were shinning bright as there was no moon. I kept looking up expecting to see a star fall or a series of stars falling. They all sat motionless. I scanned the skies looking for something to explain or match the feeling in my stomach. There was nothing that could make sense of it. Until my eyes hit the horizon and then I was reminded of an old feeling. I didn't want to believe it and in fact my mind was downright opposed to the notion. Yet, it was undeniable. There was something still missing inside of me and because of this feeling I wasn't ready to change and I wasn't ready to settle down. The horizon was still calling out to me.

But why?

I had found the fourth star so why was the horizon still calling my name? I had seen the world and back many times but why did I still feel a piece was missing inside of me? I walked back in and climbed into bed trying to forget this notion, yet I couldn't and each night the burden grew and I found it harder and harder to fall asleep.

So I did what any reasonable person would do who is lost and looking for advice. Even though it was super late, I picked up the phone and called my mother. I wanted to know if what I was feeling was normal and my mom always gave the best advice. The phone rang a few times before I heard her pick it up.

"Hello?" She said in a low muffled voice.

"Hey mum. It's me."

"Is everything alright? It's really late."

"I know it is. I just needed a bit of advice on something."

"Marry that girl."

"What? That's not why I'm calling."

"Do you need money?"

"No I don't need money."

"Oh, this can't be good. What's going on?"

"When you had me. Did you feel complete?"

"When I had you there was no doubt in my mind that being your mother is what I wanted to do and what I wanted to be."

"So, Why am I still feeling like this?"

"Feeling like what?"

"Like there's a part of me missing and the only place I can find it is out in the world."

"Can you let it go?"

"I can't even sleep."

"What do you want to do?"

"I don't know, I was kind of hoping you could give me some Motherly advice to help me figure this all out."

"Haha! Just that simple huh? Pull out some Motherly wisdom and make everything ok?"

"Yeah. Help me make sense of all of this."

"Life if filled with choices and dreams. You're old enough now make your own choices and to also follow your dreams.

Some of these things you have to give up, you got no choice in the matter. Sometimes the things you give up will haunt you till your dying days, choices you should have made but didn't. It's never easy, life never is. But my boy, you're old enough now to live your life. So make your choice but be wise."

"Thanks."

I think your Mom knew before I did. A good woman can see truth coming a mile away. Needless to say it was causing friction in our lives. We were arguing more so than ever over the most trivial of things. There was a distance growing between us and each day that divide began to thrive. She knew that it was only a matter of time before I was gone again. Her smile that I grew so fondly of, she rarely wore for me.

I lied awake looking at the ceiling trying to fall asleep but my mind always wandered back to the horizon. My mind would trace over the memories and possibilities that many more adventures were to come. But it wasn't just the adventures or the possibilities I wanted to be a part of, I was looking for me out there. The piece that would complete me and until then I found it I felt like an incomplete anxious mess.

Then I heard you scream out crying from another nightmare. I quickly got up and entered your room. You were sitting down alone with your face buried in your hands. I picked you up expecting you to want to jump out or have me take you to your Mother. With your eyes shut tight your hands touched my face, grabbed my nose and my lips. Your hand rested on my cheek.

"Dad."

You had never called me that before it stopped me in my tracks and just like that you fell back asleep in my arms. I looked at you and held you for a couple minutes watching you in slumber. Your head hit the pillow and I covered you with a blanket. When I entered the room your mother was up waiting for me, I could see the faint hint of tears across her cheeks.

"What? What is it?"

"You're going to leave us aren't you?"

"..."

"Why aren't you saying anything?"

"I don't know what to say. I'd like to stay"

"So then stay."

"I wish it were that simple."

When seeds of doubt are planted and sprout it's hard to release them it's hard to let go. A big part of me wanted to stay and a big part of me wanted to go. I was trying to make up my mind of what I wanted to do with the rest of my life. More and more I was leaning towards staying, each day when I got up and got you ready for school I wanted to stay. I loved our little family but most of all I loved being your dad. Yet the indifference between your mother and I had grown.

After school I picked you up and brought you out into the bush. I remember how scared you were of the trees and the forest when we approached them.

"Dad!" you called out as you grabbed my hand and squeezed hard.

"My boy it's okay. I'm here. I won't let anything bad happen to you."

You gave me a hug and squeezed hard and then we walked into the bush. You were still just a baby but I told you the stories of my trips to the jungle and of the fox that lied to me. We walked until it got cold and then I made a fire with you and we sat getting warm and watching it burn. You fell asleep next to the fire and I carried you home. On my way back I had made up my mind and my mind about what I was going to do and your mother had made up hers nothing was going to change it.

By the time we neared the house you had awoken jumped out of my arms and ran into the house. Dinner was already cooked and the table was set we laughed and ate and I quickly made your bed. You jumped under the covers with a storybook in hand eager to hear about an adventure. I wasn't long into reading as you drifted off to sleep. I turned the lights off and closed the door.

Your mother pulled me aside and we sat at the kitchen table. She started out the conversation with an ominous phrase that once it is spoken whatever follows is usually painful.

"We need to talk…"

"What's going on?" I asked.

She took a breath and looked deep into my eyes not once looking away.

"I don't want to be in this relationship anymore."

It hit me like a cold bucket of water to the face.

"What? Why?"

"Because I need a man who will be here no matter what. I don't have any time for doubt in me or my sons' life"

"I… I just needed some time to think."

"And that's ok with most life decisions. Being a husband and a father isn't something you should have to think about. Staying here with us should come natural. You might regret not being out there and that regret would turn into feelings of distain and animosity towards me or my son."

"I wouldn't ever have animosity towards your son. Being his Father is the greatest gift I've ever had. Giving up everything else in my life is pale in comparison."

She took a deep breath in.

"Being a father is the reward. There is nothing to sacrifice in your life. Because your life only begins to grow better each day that is spent with my son. This isn't a sudden realisation nor should you need time to convince yourself, it should just happen naturally."

I didn't know what to say.

"You shouldn't have any notion inside of leaving us… but you do don't you?"

The feeling inside my stomach kicked up again and the horizon was calling out to me. I could feel the tears coming out unmasking everything that I was trying to hide. I nodded my head and as I did I seen the tears running down the face of your mother. She didn't want me to leave either but the truth was plain as day and just as simple. She wanted a man with an unshakeable sense of belief in her and her child. She would rather face that truth head on than wait around to possibly watch it fall apart.

"In the morning it's time for you to leave." She got up walked over and gave me a kiss.

I couldn't sleep a wink. It kept going through my mind of not ever seeing you again, reading to you and being around you, it was the most empty feeling in the world. There was this loneliness inside a steadily growing hole within my heart that nothing and no one could ever fill. Heartbreak can make a sane man crazy.

Somehow I had fallen asleep.

DREAM THINGS

I was standing in a desert in the night there was no moon in the sky just stars shining brightly. In my hands was my heart and I was watching it beat. It felt warm and soft to touch, the heat it gave off was incredibly comforting. All at once it transformed and shattered into a million shards of glass that fell to the dessert floor. The warmth and comfort it brought, it brought no longer. I was scared and fearful I would lose some parts of my heart. I reached down and tried to pick them up but each piece I grabbed slid from my hands and fingers. It was like trying to grab a piece of the slipperiest Jell-o you could imagine. In my dream I had lost my heart it was no longer a part of me, the fear that I might not ever get it back terrified me greatly. In a panic the faster I tried to pick it up the more the pieces fell.

LIFE

I woke up as the sun crept in over the horizon finding its way through the curtains and beaming into the room. This was the last time I would get you ready for school. I wanted to cry and I wanted to ball my eyes out but I didn't want the last time for you to see me was with tears. I took a moment to compose myself before entering your room. I stood outside your room momentarily scanning the door, the frame and the golden knob. This was it. Then I walked in.

You were already up I could see you looking out the window.

"Dad"

"Yes my son?"

All you did was point.

"Life" I responded.

It was the last time I saw you and I remember it as if it was just yesterday. I got you ready and sent you off to school. With my bags packed I headed out the door. I didn't want to leave, I loved being a part of your life and watching you grow. I had to think of a way to win back to love and favour of your mother. Yet as I left your home my heart broke a little more with each and every breath.

LOST

I began traveling again, it didn't matter where I was or what I was doing, whenever I looked up the horizon was always calling me. Every town I visited came with a sunrise and a sunset yet I didn't care about them. I was meeting scores of different people with amazing and friendly personalities. It didn't matter. When you're in Love you see the persons face wherever you go and it's beautiful. When you're heartbroken it's the same thing but made much worse because everything is a reminder of what you once had. I had made up my mind to go back and win her favour. You see it in movies and hear it in stories about misplaced love and winning her back. The hero always wins the girl, Why couldn't that reality exist for me?
She sent me off and it was pretty clean cut and it got me thinking. Was this all a ruse? Was she doing this as a punishment or trying to teach me a lesson? I began to create scenario after scenario of returning and me sweeping her off her feet. I pictured walking into the door and dropping my bags and have her smile and then you would run up to me saying.
"Daddy"
"What took you so long?" she would say and then I would say something witty and we'd share a laugh, a smile and

a kiss. In my mind everything would right itself and we would start the rest of our lives together.

A confidence was growing that I could have her again and become your father. This time I would say to myself nothing will keep us apart. We'll have to compromise on something if I have to travel around. I mean I could always come home and we would pick up where we left off.

....Then, your Mother wrote me a letter telling me she had a new boyfriend and that they were falling in love with each other.

Along with the emptiness of heartbreak I felt a deep pain within my gut. I read and reread what she wrote me. It wasn't a letter written out of hate or anger or frustration nor was it out of sadness. I couldn't really focus on what she was trying to say in the letter, just how she ended it. *I have a new boyfriend and we're falling ... I'm sorry, I never planned for this to happen.* I read and re-read that last sentence countless times, how could I be replaced and how could I be replaced so quickly? I felt like a coat you cast aside quickly when it has served its purpose or when something better looking comes along. Like all we had shared meant nothing. There was a startling reality I had faced every day, she was moving on and yet there was nothing I could do to let you go. But I still had a sense of hope something could still be worked out between us.

...Then your Mother wrote to me and said she was engaged.

I was filled with all kinds of sadness and rage. I had the hardest time finding reasons to get up in the morning and carry on with my day. There were times where I wanted to roll over and die. I would get up half awake in the middle of the night and think I was still at your house, sleeping next to your mother and with you in the next room. Then when I sat up I realised I was alone and you weren't in the next room. I would sit awake in my bed wondering about what went wrong and what I could have done better. I felt alone in every sense of the word and there was nothing I could do to change what had happened. People often get into these places of despair in their lives for some it lasts a moment and for others they carry it until the day the die. You come to that place and it's a hard to get out of and shake off. It's an easy place to fall back into. It's a place of 'self-pity and waiting'. What are you waiting for? For a big break of course, for the lottery to choose you and for your life to just become easy without having to do any kind of work. It's a place where you can blame everyone else for everything bad that's ever happened to you. And you can wait in this place forever. I was in this place watching the years fall off the calendar. Wondering about the boy you were growing into and knowing that each day spent away you might be forgetting I was ever in your life. That thought alone was driving me crazy.

I thought about all the happiness your mother and I had shared and all our beautiful memories together. Now she was creating new memories and happiness with someone else. I couldn't help thinking why she didn't fight to keep making more memories of us together. Every day that went by I felt less as a person, the only thing that kept me going was the tiny bit of hope that somehow something would happen and I would again be your dad.

…Then she wrote to me that she was married.

I missed you so much that I cried every day to see you. I cried every day for a reality that just was no longer there. I couldn't stop what had happened and I couldn't stop myself from thinking I shouldn't have left. Nothing had any real value in my life. I had a huge gaping wound in my soul and then I tried to fill it. People do this often throughout their lives and it's something you really need to watch. Some people abuse themselves in a variety of different ways, alcohol, drugs, food and a great many others. I chose to abuse myself by dating and courting women. I wanted someone to love me and commit themselves to me in a way that your mother would have but that I rejected. Every time I had found that assurance from a female the stark realisation was that it wasn't what I wanted or needed. I broke a few too many hearts during this period of my life. Some men wear the ability to court women as a badge of honour not realising all the shame it brings in the later years of life. Nothing brought me any kind of happiness or any kind of fulfilment. I was wandering around just an empty shell of the man I was and I didn't think I could feel any worse.

...Then I was told your Mother had another child.

It's a terrible feeling to have the realisation and confirmation that the one you love has moved on without you. There was no other way to look at it. Everywhere I went I was looking to find you and every time I couldn't find you or recreate you it had me dying on the inside. Years had passed and the heartbreak of losing you didn't lessen with time every day it always felt the same. I was thinking it would never feel any better inside and that I would always carry around this loss. I hated the life I was living in.

THE BUILDING ROOM

Dreams have a funny way of letting you in on information you already knew. Like the ability to fly, is it simply because you're in a Dream that you can fly or do you just have to remember how to fly and it is the dream that gives you the answer. Dreams also help with understanding and its weird but you just know things when you dream.

I was entering the building room, the corpus with the light shining on it and the rest of the room was pitch black.

"Hey old man. Where are you?" I asked

There was no response. I was alone in the room looking at the shapeless thing on top the corpus. I stared at the corpus watching the colors change and momentarily hold and lose its shape. I leaned in close feeling frustration and anger take over.

"This whole life what have I been doing? Why have I been chasing these stars, these dreams? ALL FOR WHAT? I HAVE NOTHING BUT REMOSE AND REGRET! YOU!"

I yelled pointing my finger at the shapeless thing

"WHAT THE HELL IS SO GOD DAMNED SPECIAL ABOUT YOU? WHAT ARE YOU? I'VE SEARCHED MY WHOLE LIFE AND WHAT DO I HAVE LEFT? I'M LEFT WITH NOTHING! NOTHING! YOU KNOW WHAT YOU ARE? YOU'RE A GOD DAMNED

CURSE!"

The shapeless thing became colorless and motionless on top the corpus.

Had I killed it?

"WHAT ARE YOU?"

"I think it's time I explained what this is." The old man called out from the shadows. He walked into the light.

"What is this place? Why do you keep bringing me back here?" I asked

"I told you before that this is the Building room."

"Well... What am I building?"

"A star."

"A star?"

"Yes. You've spent your whole life creating a star, this star. It's something that will guide a very special person throughout the rest of his life. To help in the creation of this star you have to fill it but not with just good times and good memories. Stars must be forged through beauty and through pain. All the most amazing things have a heavy price, but this price is something you are gladly willing to pay for."

"You don't know that. With everything I've lost and everything I felt..."

"Your whole life you've been crafting this star for him." The old man pointed to my side.

There by my side holding my hand was you my boy. You were scared and terrified, looking at me. My emotions instantly went from rage to shame. Had you been holding my hand the whole time? I bent down and hugged you. I missed that feeling of holding you and it still felt the same. It still filled me inside. You looked up at me smiling.

"Dad."

The old man spoke and I could hear his throat break a little it seemed he was fighting off the emotions as well. Maybe he knew what I went through after all.

"It's been the most beautiful dream you've ever had. Being his father."

"..." I could feel the tears welling up. "It has been."

The old man walked over to me and placed his hand on my shoulder.

"It's time to let this dream go."

"I don't want to let him go."

"It's killing you and it will kill you if you don't let it go."

"What's he saying dad?"

I looked at the old man.

"There has to be another way."

"There is no other way if you hold onto him, onto this dream you will die and this life and all the work you've done will fade."

"I don't know what I'm supposed to do." I looked into your eyes. "What should I do?"

"Tell me about my life." You instructed

"Ok, your mother moved on when she left me and married a man and they started a family together."

"Does he love me?"

"Yeah... but I don't know, I hope he loves you the way I do."

"I never expected anyone to love me the same way. Does he love me and does he take care of me."

"Yeah. He does."

"I don't want you to die and I don't want you to hurt anymore."

"I don't know what I'm supposed to do."

"Yes you do."

I looked at the old man.

"Place him on the corpus. But don't let him go quite yet."

I grabbed you and placed you on top of it. I was holding as tightly as I could without hurting you.

"Everything you've ever done is going into this Star. It will guide him the same way the stars have guided you. It's the greatest gift a father can give to his child. It will guide him when you are not around. This whole journey has all been for him as much as it has been for you. But now your paths must split."

"What do I do now?"

"Tell him how you feel. Then let him go."
I took a deep breath as tears ran down my face.

"I've missed you so much. There is nothing out there that has been able to replace you because you are so incredibly special to me. It has a left this void in my heart and all I feel is misery and loneliness. I cried for you, every single day for a year. When times got hard I would remember the hugs and kisses you gave to me. When I am not with you I feel alone even when I am with friends and family. No matter where I am in the world, I feel alone without you in my life."

"Was it my fault you and mom never stayed together?"

"No, God no. It was never ever your fault. There are lots of reasons why things between me and your mom never worked out. Big reasons, small reasons, reasons that mattered and reasons that didn't matter, some reasons we could see and others we couldn't. But you were never ever one of those reasons that split us up. This was our fault and not yours."

"When you first came into my world it was so beautiful, innocent and carefree. I didn't know you came with a gift something that opened up every time I saw you. Every time I heard you speak and especially whenever you spoke out a new word. Every time I heard you cry especially when I could answer them holding you in my arms, I had so much love and Pride knowing that you called me Dad. Even if you were not of my blood. You have shown me that life can be so much more than what it is. "

"I have to let you go now." I said with tears running down my face. "Napi once asked me what the longest distance is with the shortest journey. This is what I have told him and what I am about to tell you. *'The longest distance with the shortest journey is the journey from your mind to your heart.'* Follow your dreams, live them the best you can and trust in spirit. I will always love you my son and that will never ever change."

"I love you too Dad."
I let go and just like that you turned into a bright shining star and joined with the shapeless thing on top the corpus. The

corpus itself morphed into an enormous shining star burning brighter than anything I had ever seen and yet even with that I could look right into it.

I learned that you have to let go of all things eventually. It doesn't always have to be a bad or terrible thing. You can let go of things in a good way. I hoped on everything that this star would guide you throughout your darkest days and loneliest nights. And just like that the star shot off into the sky and took its place in the heavens. Even though I watched it travel into the sky I couldn't remember where it went. The moment it took its place in the heavens above I instantly forgot where it was, I searched looking and trying to remember but couldn't and to this day I still can't.

The old man motioned over to me and a door opened behind him.

"There's one more thing you have to do. And it's beyond that door." He instructed.

My eyes were full of tears and he gave me a hug. I walked to the door I was trying to find a word to express how I felt but couldn't find anything. He looked at me and said.

"It's ok, you don't have say anything."

I nodded and walked through the door.

ROYALTY

I was in the desert again on my knees hovering over my shattered heart in complete desperation I was trying to pick the pieces up. But the pieces would slip through my fingers and fall and I would panic and in my panic I would speed up. Nothing. I had this incredible desire to return my heart into its place. I was tired of feeling empty and alone. I so desperately wanted it back inside. But nothing, I couldn't pick it up and the feeling of emptiness grew. I began to cry and sob and weep as I screamed out. I wanted to give up sitting there on my knees.

Have you ever met royalty? A person of great stature? They are an eloquent type of people and you can't help but feel smaller in comparison. You can't help but feel inspired and full of hope. You also can't help feeling small next to the beauty they emit.

I was sitting there full of complete desperation and hopelessness.

"What's the matter?" I heard a beautiful calming voice ask. It came from behind me and I heard footsteps walking towards.

"I lost my heart." I responded.

I turned my head around and saw this incredible sight. I was looking at a princess. She didn't look like your typical blonde haired blue eyed princess. Her skin was a beautiful shade of brown it looked warm and soft and every part of me wanted to touch, kiss and caress every part of her being. Her hair was black and beautiful flowing like a calm and chaotic river. She wasn't even wearing a white gown and tiara. She was wearing a simple black dyed buckskin dress with strange long multi-coloured feathers hanging down. She walked with grace, eloquence and power only stopping across from me and in between us was my broken heart.

"You didn't lose your heart, its right here in front of you."

"I can't pick it up. I've tried. It's impossible."

"You keep trying the same method and it's not working that doesn't mean it's impossible. It means you aren't using the right technique."

"I have no idea how else to fix my heart."

"Would you like some help?"

"Please." I felt emptiness inside "I'm completely helpless. Useless."

"No you're not you just think you are."

With that she got onto her hands and knees. I watched as she took a breath in and exhaled gently blowing onto the heart. I could see a blue mist faintly at first crawl out of her mouth that rested on the pieces, which solidified. She picked up my heart, it was still in shambles and unconnected but it was balled up in her hands.

"Are you going to fix it? Are you going to put it back together?"

"No." She said handing it over to me. "You are."

I took my broken heart back into my hands and asked.

"How do I fix it?"

She turned around and began to walk away after taking a few steps she turned her head back to me with a smile. A smile that spoke of an obvious secret, something she was about to share that was common knowledge.

"Learn to love yourself." She took a step away but stopped

herself and turned back to me. "And when you do" She raised her hand and pointed out to the heavens "Come find me."

Her brown skin began to glow and that glowed turned into a blinding light. I could hardly see her and watched as she turned into star, shooting off into the horizon. She left a trail of golden stardust that began to sparkle and shine brilliantly just for a moment and then quickly fade burning out as it fell downwards. I stood there watching the stardust gently fall blanketing the desert floor. And began to wonder if that's how the desserts of the world were created.

I awoke from the dream still hurt and still lonely and still missing you. But something was renewed inside of me and it was a feeling of hope. I remember the joy that we had and shared. That beautiful feeling was something that I could find or create and experience once again. It was the last gift you gave to me.

Dreams

EPILOGUE

Time is a funny thing and if you don't watch it, it'll pass you by so quickly. Some people lose time when traveling and others gain it when they're in a rush. And the years, well, they always fall off the calendar. It is surprising to look at the decades remembering fondly at the pain and the joy of life. All the while wondering where did all the time go. I sat down looking at the veins popping out and age spots on my tired old hands. The joints had become sore to move and my body became stiff, my hair was now a mix of grey and white. In no time at all I had become an old man.

I often take walks throughout my house reflecting on the old memories and keepsakes and other things I've had collected throughout my life. The many things I have acquired on the journeys and adventures of my life collect dust as I wipe them down. It had been ages and felt as if I was done adventuring and also felt as if I was at the last of my days.

Walking through the hallways I had come across a door that was unfamiliar it was black with white lining and had an ivory handle. I reached out and opened the door and peered in to nothing but darkness. I took a breath as I walked into the room and closed the door behind me. As it slid shut, a single light turned on shining down in the centre of the room.

The light was shining on the corpus. It looked untouched and the strange and beautiful markings still covered the concrete body.

I heard a door open and as I looked back I seen a young man enter the room. Something about this all seemed so strange and so familiar as I let out a laugh.

ABOUT THE AUTHOR

Gitz Crazyboy was born in Calgary Alberta but grew up in Fort McMurray, Alberta. He is Dene and Blackfoot, actively reconnecting to his roots. Growing up, he learned the value and power of stories from his mother, who would tell him a mixture of Dr. Seuss, Sesame Street and Blackfoot history. Throughout his life he has fallen in and out of love with reading anything and almost everything he could get his hands on. Gitz's passion is working with youth and a very close second is traveling the world. He's always looking for the peaceful spaces within the chaotic places. Along with writing Gitz loves to make and create music and always loves being introduced to new music. *"Love and Music Can Save Us."* – Anthony Keidis, is one of his favorite quotes. Gitz believes that nothing is more important than family and reconnecting back to his culture.

... MORE FROM JASON EAGLESPEAKER

AUTHENTICALLY INDIGENOUS NAPI STORIES:

Napi and the Rock
Napi and the Bullberries
Napi and the Wolves
Napi and the Buffalo
Napi and the Chickadees
Napi and the Coyote

Napi and the Elk
Napi and the Gophers
Napi and the Mice
Napi and the Prairie Chickens
Napi and the Bobcat
... and many more Napi stories

AUTHENTICALLY INDIGENOUS GRAPHIC NOVELS:

UNeducation: A Residential School Graphic Novel
Napi the Trixster: A Blackfoot Graphic Novel
UNeducation, Vol 2

AUTHENTICALLY INDIGENOUS COLORING BOOKS:

Napi: A Coloring Experience
UNeducation: A Coloring Experience
Completely Capricious Coloring Collection
A Day at the Powwow (grayscale coloring)

AUTHENTICALLY INDIGENOUS KIDS BOOKS:

Teeias Goes to a Powwow (a series)

** If you absolutely loved this book (or even just kind of liked it), please find it on AMAZON.COM and leave a quick review. Your words help more than you may realize. Thanks so much.

Find more Indigenous awesome-ness at **www.eaglespeaker.com**

CPSIA information can be obtained
at www.ICGtesting.com
Printed in the USA
LVHW05s1534290518
578848LV00010B/648/P